Protecting Joselyn
Team Cerebrus Book 1

Melissa Kay Clarke

3rd Edition

Copyright ©2018-2020 by Melissa Kay Clarke

ISBN-13: 978-1722236564
ISBN-10: 1722236566

The characters and events in this book are fictitious. Any similarity to real persons, living or dead, places, or events is coincidental and not intended by the author.

This book, or parts thereof, may not be reproduced in any form without permission. The copying, scanning, uploading, and distribution of this book via the internet or via any other means without the permission of the publisher is illegal and punishable by law. Please purchase only authorized electronic or print editions, and do not participate in or encourage piracy of copyrighted materials. Your support of the author's rights is appreciated.

Edited by Janet Poppema & Thomas "Woody" Johns

Dedication

This book is gratefully dedicated to the men and women of the
United States military - past, present, and future.

Through the best of times, you stand vigilant.
Through the worst of times, you never give up.
When others turn away, you boldly continue on.
When the strong need help, you stand in support.
When the weak cry out, you step into harm's way.

Through your selfless service,
you ensure the safety of others.
With every drop of your blood that is spilled,
you fulfill an oath.
Never back down.
Never surrender.

And we must never forget.

Thank you for your service.

Acknowledgements

Thank you, God, for the talent you have given me. I pray I will never forget from whom all blessings flow.

To my family, Robert and Rebecca, thank you for allowing me to spend all my time writing. I know you worry about me, but I think I'm alright. At least the voices in my head say so - when they aren't arguing.

For the MKC Beta Brigade: Donna, Jon, Hannah, and Holly. Once again, I couldn't have done this without your invaluable help. Thank you for keeping me on track and focused. I appreciate every hint, argument, suggestion, and virtual butt kicking you have given me. Your advice is invaluable and your support priceless.

Lastly, I want to thank my readers. If it weren't for you, I wouldn't have anyone to tell my little stories to. Thank you for giving me a chance. I am humbled and eternally grateful.

Prologue

*T*here were too many bodies shoved into the space, causing the overwhelmed air conditioning system in the ancient courthouse to groan. Late spring in Pensacola could be warm at times, but given the unusual temperature spike for April, it felt more like the midst of summer. Even the oppressive heat couldn't keep the gawkers away today. People were tightly packed into the hard wooden bench seats with even more people crowded around the walls. The air was charged with electrical energy, and a nervous buzz filled the room.

The loud slam of wood on wood echoed through the courthouse as Judge David Rockwell called the room to order. Whispers slowly died out as all attention turned to the eight men and four women sitting quietly in the box to the judge's left.

"In the matter of the State of Florida versus Douglas Beecher McClane, Madam Foreman, has the jury reached a decision?"

The woman, Joselyn Kendrik, stood in front of the seat marked with a black number seven on the back. "Yes, your honor, we have," she said staring resolutely at the judge. Throughout the proceedings, she had been stoic, listening and making the occasional notes on a pad in her lap. Though she was only twenty-three, she had been chosen as foreman because of her ability to keep a cool head, not to mention the pre-law degree she obtained last year. Her ability to explain certain nuances of the law to the others had been priceless.

Now the bulk of the trial was over. There seemed to be a restless demeanor about her as if she couldn't wait to get it finished. She pressed a piece of folded paper into the bailiff's waiting hand and stood with her fingertips against the bar before her. The paper was delivered to Judge Rockwell who read it then had it returned to her. Clutching the verdict in her fingers, she faced the courtroom and waited as Judge Rockwell made notes on a pad on his desk.

Nervously glancing at the cold, stony countenance of the former school teacher and accused rapist and murderer, Joselyn paled to find those hard hazel eyes boring into her. She had made it a point throughout the proceedings to only glance at him quickly to observe his attitude as the grisly details of each heinous act were explained. Throughout it all, he had remained aloof, as if nothing could touch him. Now he stared at her unabashedly. At his side, his attorney leaned over and whispered something into his ear. With a slow wink, McClane turned his baleful gaze back to the judge, breaking their locked stares and freeing her to focus on Judge Rockwell's words as he began to explain the coming procedure and what was expected. Smoothing her fingers over the deep amethyst of her dress, she listened to the judge as he arrived at the verdict portion of his spiel.

One by one, he read the twenty-three charges. Twenty-three heinous acts of horror perpetrated against six victims. Some of the crime scene photographs had been so ghastly; two jurors had become physically ill. The evidence was overwhelming, and it only took six hours of deliberation to reach the unanimous decision. Guilty.

With the last verdict stated, a loud shout lifted into the air, and several reporters rushed out of the courtroom. Judge Rockwell banged his gavel again, and the noise dropped. Quickly, he polled the jury to confirm they each agreed with the verdict. Once completed, he turned his gaze to the smirking man whose dead, staring eyes were fixed on Joselyn's face.

"Mr. McClane, you have been found guilty of all twenty-three charges by a jury of your peers. Sentencing will be in three days." He raised his gavel to dismiss the courtroom when Douglas McClane suddenly leaped over the table and threw himself at Joselyn. His momentum was stopped when his chest hit the bar. He stood there, glaring at her horrified face and clenching the wood with his fingers. Leaning forward, he screamed at her, flecks of spittle flying through the air as she drew back in fear.

"Six blooms,
Six goodbyes,
Six voices,
Six sighs.
Six slashes,
Six cries,
Seven strokes,
Seven will die."

Pandemonium broke out as two burly bailiffs grabbed Douglas McClane's arms, yanking him away from the juror's box and down to the floor on his stomach. As the judge banged his gavel in an attempt to regain control of the situation, cuffs were produced and placed on the newly convicted criminal's wrists. Pulling him upright again, the bailiffs and two sheriff's deputies dragged him toward the door.

Joselyn sat in stunned silence, her face a pale ghostly white in stark contrast to her vibrant purple dress. Her fist still clutched the piece of folded paper as she watched them manhandle McClane through the door. The jury was dismissed, and the judge disappeared through a different door, but she didn't move. In her mind, McClane's final shrill words assaulted her as he was removed from the room.

"I'll see you soon, Little Rose. My garden still needs tending."

Chapter 1

Soul crushing was the perfect way to describe the weight of dread pressing upon Joselyn as she sat in a folding chair facing a large, file-covered desk. The office was on the small side with gray walls and cracked linoleum popular about forty years ago. Overhead, the ceiling sported a large mustard-colored stain directly above the desk that most likely came from years of cigarette smoke. She stared at the spot and fought to bring her raging emotions under control as the man occupying the desk sealed her fate.

"I'm sorry, Ma'am, but there's nothing we can do."

She was tired, cranky and scared; emotions which triggered her inner snark and it came out with a vengeance. "What do you mean there's nothing you can do? You're the police, are you not? Your whole 'serve and protect' motto is even written on your cars, isn't it, Detective Jameson?"

The middle-aged police detective dropped his face into his hand and scrubbed the salt and pepper scruff there. He seemed to be in his early fifties but still in great shape. If she were to be honest with herself, she didn't know many men her age who were as defined as this man. He must either work out like crazy or have perfect genes and metabolism to be this buff.

Taking a deep breath, he tried again. "You don't

seem to understand the problem here."

Her eyes narrowed as she glared at him. "No, I don't think *you* understand the problem here." She placed the black box on top of a stack of reports and pointed at it. "My life is in danger."

Detective Jameson glanced into the box and shook his head. "Just because someone gives you a gift doesn't mean they are trying to kill you. Most girls would be thrilled to have a secret admirer. You have to admit being who you are; it's to be expected."

She ignored the patronizing tone when he said 'girls' and stuck her hand into the box. Pulling out a clear container, she dropped it on the desktop.

He looked at the package containing seven of the plumpest strawberries ever seen wrapped in milk chocolate and decorated with white dots. "I..."

She huffed and leaned over the desk. "Wait, let me explain this to you again, Detective Jameson. As I told you, I'm deathly allergic to both strawberries and chocolate. This 'gift' contains both. It's a time bomb waiting for me!"

Confusion washed over his face, and he gaped at her. "Lots of people have food allergies, and you can't expect everyone to know what yours are. It's a bad choice of gift, I agree, but it doesn't mean the sender is out to kill you. You have to see reason here." Standing slowly, he picked up the carton and placed it back into the box. Pushing it into her hands, he said tiredly, "Throw it away. You have to understand this is part of being a bestselling author. Not only are you an attractive young lady, but you also have a lot of fans. This also means you're going to get attention."

She ignored his attempt to placate her. "Attention? You call this attention. Maybe I have written a few books people like and buy. I didn't even... You don't... This is..." She growled in frustration. "I make my living using words, and I can't even get you to understand." The helplessness of her situation dampened her fury until it evaporated. She felt the tears pooling in her eyes but refused to let them fall. Placing the box on the floor at her feet she sunk into the chair once again. Taking a haggard breath, she tried one more time.

"Yes, I get gifts all the time. Things from my readers are the norm. I receive key chains, pictures...the occasional coffee mug. You see, my heroine, Deidre Cole, collects coffee mugs. Consequently, my readers send me quirky ones they find. I love that they connect to her on such a level." The brief smile left her face as she steered her thoughts back to the subject at hand. "However, that's not the point."

She stopped and chewed her lip a moment before continuing. "Let me put it into perspective. Say this had been one of those fruit arrangement things or cookies or even something else. Anything other than chocolate covered strawberries. I would have assumed it came from my mother and eaten half of it without thinking. Anything else in this world and I wouldn't have thought twice about it. However, my mom and anyone else who knows me would also know about my allergy so getting this particular gift set off red flags. No, Detective Jameson, this came from someone else, and I know who it was. I'm alive and sitting here right now because Douglas Beecher McClane doesn't know I'm allergic."

A confused frown wrinkled his brow. Sitting back, he tucked his hands behind his neck, dropped his chin and glanced at her over the rim of his reading glasses. "I still can't understand why you would think this was anything other than a mistake. Wait... Douglas Beecher McClane?" His eyebrows raised as understanding dawned. "You mean the serial rapist and murderer? The one they called 'The Gardener?'"

Clutching her fingers tightly, she twisted them as she cleared her throat. "The same," she choked out. "You see, Detective Jameson, Chambers is a pen name. My real name is Joselyn Kendrik. I was the foreman for his trial."

The shock almost knocked him off his seat. "You're Joselyn Kendrik, 'the' Joselyn Kendrik? The one he called 'Little Rose'... the woman he fixated on following his trial and escape? I remember the manhunt for him. I got a lot of overtime every time someone swore they saw him in New Orleans." Detective Jameson threw up his hands. "Okay, I can see now why you might freak out a little. I mean, getting a half dozen blood covered roses on Valentine's day from an escaped murderer-rapist would make anyone a little paranoid. The only problem is he can't have sent you anything. He's dead."

She ignored his last comment. "To borrow from a common saying, I'm not paranoid if I know he is coming to get me." She raised her gaze and bit her lip. "I know you've seen the footage. You must have.

Everyone has!"

The news bite from Douglas McClane's verdict reading made a big splash on both local and national news. There were not supposed to be any cameras in the courtroom, but someone had taken a grainy four-minute video using a cell phone. Though the quality was poor, the look of sheer terror on her face was quite clear when Douglas McClane lunged at her, spouting his impromptu poetry. They had even managed to record his screamed promise as he was dragged from the courtroom. The video went viral within minutes of being uploaded to YouTube. She shuddered every time she saw it.

"Nobody took it too seriously. Not at first, anyway. He was locked away in prison, waiting on death row. I remember watching the news when the story broke of him escaping during a prison transfer. It never occurred to me he would try to follow through on his promise from the courtroom." She shivered. "But those roses came along with its poem and suddenly my life was turned upside down." Closing her eyes, she recited the words burned into her retinas.

Roses are red
Or so goes the rhyme
Pink and white blossoms
On trellises do climb.
But my Rose has hair
The color of silk
Eyes of sweet caramel
And skin like milk.
So beautiful to pluck
As she blooms on a vine

*Essence deep red
Like the finest of wine.
My Rose, sweet Joselyn
Her time draws near
To be taken, consumed
As I feast on her fear.*

She opened her eyes; her face was frozen in a pained expression before continuing. "The police were able to positively identify the blood as coming from Douglas McClane, so I was whisked away into witness protection where I stayed for three long years. You have no idea how relieved I was when Jonathan, my handler, got a call informing us McClane was dead. I wanted to see the body in person to try and regain some of my equilibrium back, but my therapist talked me out of it. She said he had already taken too much from me and I would be giving him more control in death. I needed to move on, get back into my life." She snorted. "Easier said than done. They did let me see the pictures of the crime scene, so I was able to get some closure. Finally, I could reclaim my life, but the time I spent in hiding changed me. I didn't want to go into law any longer; my experiences soured me on becoming an attorney. Instead, I took all the anger, fear and worry and turned it into words, pages, and stories. Three books in nine months, Detective Jameson. It is the legacy Douglas McClane left me. He was dead and gone, but I have *The Deidre Files* and a bright new future awaiting me. So imagine my surprise when I came home from a writer's conference yesterday to find this box on my doorstep. He had been there, at *my* house. A man who tortured, raped and murdered six women had stood on *my* front step, in a protected, gated community long enough to leave me a box."

He sighed. "Ms. Chambers, ah, I mean Ms. Kendrik." He hesitated a moment, "Which do you prefer?"

"Kendrik is fine."

"Ms. Kendrik, I can understand your concern, and if I were you, I'd take up the issue of unwanted deliveries with your homeowner association. However, the fact remains McClane is dead. If you feel this incident is related, why didn't you call your handlers in Witness Protection?"

"You think I didn't? I called Jonathan first thing, and he told me I was paranoid. He said a dead man can't be sending me gifts and told me it was probably from a fan."

He didn't say anything just nodded in agreement.

Frustration made her want to scream. Throwing her head back, she closed her eyes and silently counted to ten. Finally finding a bit of calm, she lowered her head, opened her eyes, unfurled her fists and winced to see half moon imprints in her palm from her fingernails.

He continued as if he didn't notice her. "If I remember correctly, he was killed by the police in a cemetery in Florida?"

She nodded. "The same one that contains my father's grave. He was putting a slashed stuffed bear wearing a purple dress on his tombstone when they caught him. A groundskeeper saw him and reported it."

The frustration was clear on his face. "Okay, but he's dead. I remember it clearly when the news came down the line. First time in two years I got to take a full week's vacation. Unless I'm missing something here, he's gone, Ms. Kendrik, dead. Ghosts can't hurt you, and that's what Douglas McClane would have to be. It's impossible for him to have sent you a box of strawberries yesterday."

"I thought so too, but he's not. He's out there somewhere." She pulled out a piece of folded paper and slid it across the cluttered desktop. "This was hidden in the box, under the tissue paper. I didn't see it until later."

He unfolded the paper and read the words.

Roses are bloody
Beware the thorns.
Veratrum is poison
In all of its forms.
Cacti have blooms
But also have stings.
Death will come knocking
Carrying beautiful things.

"It's almost verbatim to the poem I found on my father's grave last year. I never told anyone about it because, frankly, Detective Jameson, I saw was no reason to as he was dead. The only difference is the line 'Roses are bloody.' The original said 'Roses bear beauty.' The bloody part is a direct reference to the first gift he gave me. Before you say anything, yes, the words may not be the same, but yet they are. I promise you, if a murdering rapist leaves you a love poem, you don't forget even a single word of it.

EVER! I don't know how, why or where, but I assure you, Detective Jameson, he still wants to keep his promised date with me, and I don't have much time before he comes to collect me in person."

He pulled out a rubber glove and took the paper from her. "I'll have this checked for fingerprints, but I can almost guarantee you there's nothing there." He placed the letter into a small bag and wrote on the front. Tapping his pen on his desk, he collected his thoughts. "Look, I'll open a case file containing this evidence in a possible stalker situation, but there's nothing else I can do. It's not like I can put out an APB for a dead man. I'll tag it as a potential copycat."

"It's not a copycat; it's him. I can't explain to you exactly how I know, but it is. This is Douglas McClane. I know it deep inside." She stood, retrieved the box and dropped it into the garbage can next to his desk. Turning, she went to the door of his office and looked back. "Go ahead and open the stalker file but I don't believe it will make any difference. After I'm murdered, maybe you can get him before he kills again. At least my death would have a purpose." Without a backward glance, she exited his office and disappeared.

Chapter 2

*M*addox "River" Benson twirled the long neck beer between his hands, causing droplets of condensation to fly in a graceful arc to the table top and soak into the napkin bearing the bar logo. He frowned when the thin paper tore, and he pushed it into a small sodden pile next to the empty bottles in the center.

"So, what are you going to do now you're retiring?"

He glanced at the assembled men sitting at the large table. Grayson Titus, Alcide Montgomery, Levi Salter, Reese Harkins and Asher Finchly looked at him expectantly. The team of SEALs, also known as Bruiser, Cowboy, Hick, Toad and Finch were some of the best men he had ever had the pleasure to know through the years. He was close to his team; SEALs were all brothers-in-arms and saw to it they always had each other's six. One couldn't go through everything they had and not feel a sense of family.

"I got a couple of things banging around in my head." He took a draw on the beer, pulled the label off and flashed the group a half smile. "I'll figure something out."

The pretty waitress bent over the table and placed the bottles on her tray. "Another round?" she asked. He shook his head and tilted the still quarter full bottle slightly. She smiled but suddenly lurched forward. "Hey, watch it!" she shouted over her shoulder.

Every man at the table, the entire SEAL team, stiffened and stared at the men. Cowboy cleared his throat and raised one eyebrow at the boisterous group. Catching the glares, the men murmured a quick apology and hurried to the other side of the packed room. "My heroes," the waitress murmured before returning to the bar with her loaded tray.

"So, River, how did you get your nickname?" The pretty blonde sitting on Toad's lap asked. "I've heard a lot of stories about how some guys get names and 'River' seems a little unique."

"Not a lot to say really. I was born and raised in Mississippi. You know, Mississippi River." He shrugged. "Could be worse."

"It almost was," Bruiser chuckled. "Something about strong hands and working on a farm."

"Yeah, something like it," River growled and sat his beer on the table. "There was no way I was going to let y'all saddle me with a name referencing a cow's body part. I wasn't particularly tickled about 'River' either but considering the alternative, it worked." He shrugged. "Now the name had grown on me, and for the most part, I prefer it to Maddox."

"Well, I like it," she gave him a winning smile as she ran her fingers through the scruff on Toad's cheek. "It's strong."

River took the opportunity to change the subject. "Any news on who's replacing me?"

Bruiser shook his head. "Dixon hasn't given me any info yet. We'll probably get whoever it is in the next few days," he added. "Going to take a big man to replace you, River."

"Yeah, who's going to keep Toad in line?" Hick asked. "He's already a handful."

"Hey," Toad grumbled as he lifted his date out of his lap. "I resent that. I'm not a handful, thank you."

"I disagree," the blonde purred. "You're more than a handful." She waggled her eyebrows suggestively as she wrapped her arms around his waist. "Definitely a handful and then some."

"And on that note, I'm outta here. River, have a good life; don't be a stranger. The rest of you, I'll see tomorrow." Toad placed his hand on his date's back and gently guided her out the door.

"Jesus," Finch muttered.

River threw his hands up in mock surrender. "And just when I thought there wasn't anything I was going to miss about being in the SEALs."

They all laughed, and River turned his thoughts inward. He took another drink of his beer and watched the dynamics of the group. It was obvious to anyone how close they were and regardless of what he had said, he felt a twinge of loss knowing he would no longer be a part of the team. Soon, the others would be off on a mission, and he'd be left behind. He sighed heavily as the weight of his new situation bore down on him. Sitting here was making him more nostalgic. What was he thinking coming here on his last night in Coronado? He should be in his apartment getting ready to leave. The furniture rental company had already come by yesterday, so there were only a few things left. Other than his clothes and a handful of odds and ends he'd collected over the years, nothing else remained. He was leaving in the morning; leaving a life he had known for the past twenty years and heading into what? When he said he had something in mind, it hadn't been exactly true. The only thing he had planned was a visit to his family. Twenty years in the service, including twelve as a member of the elite SEALs teams, and now he didn't know what would be next in his life. There was little call for trained snipers in the outside world and although he had the college bill to use, going to college at thirty-eight didn't sound appetizing either.

Looking around at the team laughing together made something clench in his gut. It was going to be hard acclimating to life after the SEALs. He knew he was lucky in leaving with body intact and only a handful of scars both inside and out. Some things would haunt him in the night, but he knew of too many brothers who had returned from missions severely altered by what they had seen and done. Add that to the others who never came back, and he felt fortunate, indeed. Finding the current stream of his thoughts too maudlin, he rubbed his hand over his face, pulled a bill from his pocket and tossed it on the table before standing.

"Are you leaving already?" Every eye at the table was trained on him.

He nodded. "Yeah, I got a long drive tomorrow, so I better get some rest."

As one every man stood and solemnly shook his hand before giving him a manly half-hug. Murmurs of "take care" and "see ya" drifted around the room.

As he turned, he heard, "Once a SEAL..." He looked back to see Cowboy lift his beer.

"Always a SEAL," the others finished in unison before lifting their beers in a salute. River snagged his and downed the last swallow. These were his brothers, his closest friends, and it was difficult to walk away. He knew without a doubt if any of them ever needed him, he'd be there and the same was true for them. SEALs never left SEALs behind.

Making his way out through the crowd, he felt his cell vibrate in his pocket. Fishing it out, he glanced at the caller ID and frowned. Who would be calling him from New Orleans? Stepping out of the noise and onto the sandy beach, he connected the call. "Yeah?"

"River, I need your help."

River was shocked when he recognized the voice of his former team member and unofficial leader, Henry Jameson.

"Bull? Jesus man, it's been what, six years? How the hell are you?"

"Tired."

River chuckled. "I was wondering who was calling from New Orleans Police Department. Do you need bail money?"

"Nah, I'm working here; got my detective shield a few years back, which is why I'm calling. You got a minute?"

"I got all the time you need."

"Yeah, I talked to Bruiser earlier today. He told me you were exiting so I was hoping you could help me. I need to call in a solid if you have some time and don't have anything planned for a few days."

"I'm free. What's up?"

"How fast can you get to New Orleans?"

Chapter 3

*J*oselyn stared at her plate of scrambled eggs and bacon with disgust. She dropped her fork and pushed it away. This constant worrying she was suffering had all but killed her appetite.

She pulled her laptop out, placed it carefully on the table and pressed the start button. The whine of the fans from the aging cooling pad underneath reminded her she needed to get a new one soon. Mentally, she added a trip to the electronics store to her growing to-do list. Glancing around the coffee shop from the corner booth, she dropped her attention to the screen and attempted to lose herself in the universe of her latest novel.

A sound caught her attention, pulling her from the world in which she was immersed. Two rather large men stood beside her table, and she barely managed to stifle a scream before recognizing one as Detective Jameson. Flicking her gaze to his companion, she realized she had never seen this one before. The detective was intimidating, but he was nothing compared to the man beside him. There was something insanely dangerous about him, something she couldn't quite put her finger on. The man radiated an aura of deadly power, and she had to fight pulling away from them in defense. He reminded her of a wild animal; keep your distance and you were safe but get too close to him or his territory, and you would regret it. He stood at least six feet tall with broad shoulders rippling with muscle. He had well-defined arms and a trim waist emphasized by his tight jeans. The material of his dark tee shirt was stretched tightly over his torso and tucked into his waistband. His definition was not that of a professional bodybuilder but was clearly a man who was accustomed to working hard with his entire body. His strong, calloused hands caught her attention. Her thoughts on how it would feel to have him holding her with those hands splayed against her back sent flashes of heat through her. She watched mesmerized as his right hand lifted and plucked the dark sunglasses from his face. His raven black hair was a little long, but it along with his tanned face showcased some of the palest blue eyes she'd ever seen. Beneath them, she observed his straight, Romanesque nose, wide cheekbones and square chin covered in dark stubble. Either his facial hair grew quickly, or he hadn't shaved in a few days. Something told her the latter must be the case.

She was floored. His mixture of danger and stunning looks made her want to dive into his eyes and never come out. As for his body, she wanted to run her hands over every ripple and dip until she could draw his form in her dreams. It seemed as if he could read her thoughts when one corner of his mouth twitched into a smile. Before she could stop herself, she licked her lips and blushed, trying to look away before he realized she had been undressing him with her mind only moments before.

"May we join you, Ms. Kendrik?"

Startled out of her daydream, she recovered and

motioned toward the cracked vinyl seat across from her. "Detective Jameson, good to see you again."

Immediately, a waitress appeared at the table, eyes glued to Detective Jameson's companion sitting ramrod straight across from her. "Hey darlin', I'm Helen. What can I get for you?"

"Coffee," they said in unison.

Darting off to the counter, she returned only moments later placing two cups of rich, black brew in front of them. With a wink, she dropped a container of creamer beside. "Sugar's on the table. What else can I get you?" Her eyes were devouring the stranger with promises of what else he could easily have, and not necessarily from the menu. Joselyn rolled her eyes. Helen was so cliché it was positively funny.

"Coffee is enough," Detective Jameson smiled but waved her off. With a pout on her cherry red lips, Helen sashayed to the front with an exaggerated sway of her narrow hips. Stopping to look over her shoulder, she realized neither of the men was paying her any attention. With a huff, she pushed through the door and disappeared into the back. Joselyn snorted. She couldn't stand women who relied on blatant sexual innuendos to grab a man's attention.

Completely oblivious to the scene that just transpired, Detective Jameson took a sip of the black drink and winced at the bitter brew. Tossing in some sugar, he tried it again and nodded. Next to him, his friend took his black. She studied the man again for a moment. Even though his hair was dark instead of Viking blond, he reminded her of the old Norse legends of the Frost Giants. Cold. Impassive.

Untouchable. Yes, the moniker seemed to fit him pretty well.

"Ms. Kendrik, Joselyn, I believe I owe you somewhat of an apology." Detective Jameson shot her a sheepish glance.

"Excuse me?" She frowned in confusion. "Why do you owe me an apology?"

He rubbed his bottom lip with the corner of his thumbnail and grimaced.

"Yeah, okay. Here goes," Jameson muttered. "After you left my office, I couldn't stop thinking about this whole situation and the more I thought about it, the more wrong it felt. I learned a long time ago to trust my instincts, so I dug out the box of strawberries and looked it over carefully. Nothing appeared wrong, just strawberries and chocolate like you buy at the store. In fact, with Mother's day coming soon, you can find these in any grocery store in the city. It looked like a sweet attempt by some unknown person to impress someone they liked. Don't get me wrong - it's never a good idea to eat something sent to you by a stranger but it seemed innocuous enough. As I was about to drop them back into the trash, I saw it. On one of the strawberries was a little hole in the chocolate - a tiny puncture. Now, it could have been from a bubble popping when the chocolate cooled, but my intuition said it was something more sinister. I sent it in to be checked, and you know what they found? It had been injected with ketamine - enough to knock a linebacker down." He flashed her a pained look. "Good thing you're allergic, eh? Had you eaten it, there's no telling where you would be now or what would have happened. In a nutshell, you were right. You do have a reason to be concerned."

She gasped as her eyes widened. Having her fears suddenly confirmed should have filled her with a sense of vindication. It didn't. Instead, her heart started to pound, and her hands became sweaty. Someone had tried to slip her tranquilizers. The ramifications weren't lost on her.

"Unfortunately, ketamine is extremely easy to get - the streets are full of it, so there's no way to track it. I took all the evidence including the toxicology report along with your statement to my captain. While he agrees there is a reason for concern, he won't even entertain the idea it could be Douglas Beecher McClane. I even went so far as to contact the detective in charge of his case in Pensacola to ensure there is no way McClane could still be alive and kicking. He assured me - Douglas McClane is dead, without any doubt at all. So officially, it's an assault attempt by an unknown person. We have opened a file for you, but otherwise, there's not much we can do until we have concrete, non-dead name to go into it."

"Great. You agree I'm in danger but can't do anything about it. What am I supposed to do?" Her words were full of defeat. At least now he was listening to her. Too bad it didn't seem to matter, anyway.

"I asked my captain the same thing, and he suggested a personal bodyguard. After mulling it over, I agree with him. You're a celebrity of sorts. Minor, perhaps but enough of one that you deserve personalized attention. You could hire a firm to take over, but sometimes they are too wrapped up in catering to big-name clients and smaller, less significant ones slip through their fingers. I felt guilty about brushing you off earlier and knowing what I do about the strawberries I want to make it up to you." Gesturing to the man beside him, Detective Jameson announced, "Ms. Joselyn Kendrik, meet Maddox Benson. Everyone calls him 'River.' River and I go back to my time in the military. Now, he's going to help me keep you from getting hurt. You can dismiss my suggestion and hire your own team, but you can't do better than River. He's highly trained and skilled in security measures as well as personal safety."

Joselyn looked skeptical. "Help you? What exactly does that mean since I gather you aren't exactly allowed to do anything officially?"

"Yeah, about that." He looked uncomfortable. "I've been keeping an eye on you for the last week." He hurried to lift his hands. "Not in a creepy way but to make sure neither of us was paranoid." He barked out a half laugh. "As you said, you aren't paranoid if they really are out to get you. I thought everything was fine until I got pulled into my captain's office a couple of days ago. He tells me he received an anonymous call from one of your neighbors complaining about me hanging around. I'm not sure how they knew it was me since I was on personal time and using my private vehicle. I've been told to stay away from you. He motioned to the three of them sitting at the table, "This is the extent of my allowed contact with you. Strictly a social meeting, nothing official."

"I can't believe one of my neighbors tried to get you into trouble. Our neighborhood is very quiet, and people mind their own business. It's one of the reasons I purchased a house there." Joselyn protested.

He leaned forward and lowered his voice. "Joselyn, I'm pretty sure it wasn't a neighbor. Because of my gut feeling, I've ignored orders and kept an eye on you anyway."

The Frost Giant glanced at Detective Jameson and raised an eye. Henry ignored him and continued.

"Then something happened." Detective Jameson continued. Pulling out his cell, he fiddled with the buttons before turning the screen toward her. She took it and concentrated on the screen before letting out a gasp of dismay. There was a picture of a dark blue sedan sitting in what was obviously a parking lot. Four words were written across the windshield in red.

The Rose is mine.

Joselyn felt a chill race up her back, and the phone dropped from her nerveless fingers.

Detective Jameson caught it and slid it into his pants pocket. "I found that little love note on my car two days ago. *My* car, Joselyn. The writing matches the note left with your strawberries. Whoever this guy is, he has big brass balls to vandalize a car sitting in the parking lot at the precinct. In my book, it makes him either certifiably insane or undeniably stupid, and neither sits well with me. Unfortunately, until this nut job makes a move against you and we catch him at it, we can't do anything. My hands are officially tied. But

I refuse to stand by and let you get hurt by this sick bastard. I spent too many years in too many hell holes preventing the dregs of society from performing unspeakable atrocities against their fellow man to let it go. Not happening, not on my watch. So I found someone who will be able to stick with you while I work the official channels. I trust him with my life but most importantly, I trust him with yours. Will you accept my suggestion? Will you let River keep you safe?"

It was all too much to take in at one time. Later, when she had time to digest this pile of information thrown at her, she would have the mental breakdown she deserved. But for now, she simply nodded. "Okay."

His shoulders relaxed as he reached over and patted her hand gently. "Good. Try to let River take care of you. He's a good man, and I wouldn't have him here if I didn't believe in him. Listen to him; he won't do anything to hurt you." Detective Jameson stood and gripped his friend on the shoulder. "I'll be in touch." He turned and strolled out of the door.

Her new bodyguard was in the military? No wonder he seemed both protective and dangerous. She studied him for a moment as he stared at her with an unreadable expression on his face. "So..." she said nervously.

He stopped her with a slash of his hand. "Ms. Kendrik, let's get this out of the way. Bull and I served together in the Navy. He's a brother who I'll do anything for, so when he called, I came. He briefed me on the situation on the way here about the threat to your life. That is the only reason I'm here. I'm to ensure you have the best security possible. I saw the way you looked at me, and I can guess what was going through your mind because I've seen that look before. Forget it. My concern begins and ends with your safety. Period. I'm not here to be your friend or your confidant. I have no interest in finding out anything about your life other than what is strictly necessary to keep you safe. You're a job, and I'm a means to an end. When this creep is taken care of, and I'm no longer needed, I'll be leaving. Therefore, whatever romantic notion you're entertaining about us, forget it. Listen to my advice, do what I say, and you'll come out of this unharmed." He slid the sunglasses out from the neck of his shirt and pushed them on his face. "With that out of the way, and if you're ready, I need to evaluate the security of your environment. The sooner I get a grip on things, the better." Standing, he waited beside the table, feet shoulder-width apart and hands clasped behind his back. He raised one eyebrow at her as if to say, *Well?*

White hot fury washed over Joselyn like a tsunami. How dare he lump her in the same category as Helen, the waitress? He made it clear in his little diatribe what he thought of her and this whole insane situation. Yeah, her life was pretty craptastic at the moment, and perhaps she was guilty of having a few improper thoughts, but that didn't give him the right to say such harsh things to her. She was the one being pursued by a deranged stalker. All she did was perform her civic obligation and serve when called. He was military. Surely he comprehended performing a duty, so was it too much to ask for a little understanding? The tiniest bit of kindness? But no, here she sat, gawking at an impenetrable wall of muscles and bad attitude. Her first impression was right. He was a Frost Giant. Right now, she was too ticked off and way too exhausted to address his rude comments but she would soon. The only reason she wasn't sending his rather impressive butt packing was that Detective Jameson vouched for him. She was tired of being scared and on edge all the time. Straightening her spine, she glared at him and closed her laptop. With a quick shove, she pushed it into her bag and stood. Tossing the strap over her shoulder, she swayed when the overstuffed satchel pulled her off balance. River's hand shot out to steady her, and she yanked away from his touch angrily. "I'm fine," she hissed. Tossing a wadded up ten on the table, she lifted her chin arrogantly and stormed toward the door. Although she didn't look behind her, she knew the Frost Giant followed.

She didn't want to admit it, but she already felt safer.

River's eyes were glued to the gentle swing of the most perfect rump he had ever had the privilege to watch. Okay, he admitted it, he was a butt man, and damn if Joselyn Kendrik's derriere wouldn't make a monk sit up and take notice. Dark wash jeans stretched over her perfect heart shaped bottom, cupping it gently as she sashayed out of the room. Letting his gaze travel slowly upwards, he took in her hourglass shape, dainty shoulders and graceful neck. Long hair the color of spun honey caught in an elastic hair thing making a high ponytail touch the base of her neck. Once it was down, he knew it would spill over her shoulders and brush the tops of her perfect breasts. Up until now, he had always favored brunettes, but her color blonde called to him. When she looked up at him from that corner table with those big whiskey brown eyes, he felt a twinge of desire. She was breathtaking! Forgoing the layers of makeup that most women seem to favor these days, Joselyn's natural beauty took him by surprise. Until that moment, he would have sworn that he didn't like freckles, but now they were his favorite adornment. Realizing it would be difficult for him to adequately keep his mind on his duty and not on her, he steeled himself and denied the growing attraction. Damn it! He couldn't get involved, not when the object of his infatuation was in trouble and needed all of his faculties to keep her alive. Bull had sent him copies of all the files. He had his telephone app read the information to him on the thirty hour trip from California. After all she had been through, there was no way he would subject her to more groping and pawing. His eyes followed the beauty sauntering in front of him and growled. His harsh monologue had been for his benefit as much as for hers. He needed to nip the obvious mutual attraction in the bud before it had a chance to take root. An angry Joselyn would keep him out of her thoughts which, in turn, would make his job easier. He could do this. No, he *would* do this, because the alternative was not acceptable. He would protect her with his life. It may not be Douglas McClane stalking her but whoever it was would not get his hands on her.

Suddenly, Joselyn stopped in front of him to pull the door open. He stepped to the side, grabbed the handle and held it for her. She looked straightforward, marching through the door and onto the sidewalk. He followed, his eyes again dropping to examine her rear. He couldn't help but grin. Tamping down his libido, he buried his attraction and took in their surroundings. Time to get to work.

She stepped off the sidewalk and into the lot where he had met Bull earlier. Weaving through the cars, she stopped quickly. River barely avoided bumping into her. Taking a step back, he forced himself to sweep the area again rather than concentrate on Joselyn as she bent over to retrieve a key ring she dropped. He bit back a groan. Fate hated him. There was no other reason for the torment he was currently suffering. Forcing Joselyn's beauty from his mind, he looked past her to the little silver smart car she was currently unlocking.

Oh, *hell* no.

"Uh."

Whirling around, she slammed her fists on her hips and stared at him. "What?"

Even in that defensive stance, she was so adorable. Clearing his throat, he gestured toward the tiny car. "I'll never fit in that thing. Lady, I have boots bigger than your tin can. We'll take my truck, and I'll ask Bull to send someone to pick yours up."

"No can do, Mr. Benson." Twirling around, she slid into the seat and slammed the door. Cracking the window slightly, she called out. "You can follow me to my house, or you can get the address from Detective Jameson, but I'm leaving now in my baby.

Stay or go, whichever you prefer."

He opened his mouth to argue, but she glared at him, rolled up the window, shoved a pair of dark pink sunglasses on her face and started the car. He snorted at the wimpy whine the hybrid engine made and shook his head. Something told him she would follow through on her threat to leave him behind, so he quickly jogged to his black Ford F-250 truck. Opening it with the fob, he slid in, buckled the seatbelt and started the engine. River realized it would look a bit childish, but he couldn't resist revving his motor. For some perverse reason, he found a certain satisfaction in the eye roll Joselyn shot him. Surprisingly, she had waited for him. Motioning for her to lead on, he pulled behind her, followed her out of the lot and onto the road. He chuckled. This was not at all what he had thought his first job out of the Navy would be but he couldn't complain. Since his "office" came with a daily view of Joselyn, maybe retirement wouldn't be so bad after all.

Chapter 4

*T*he nerve of him!

Later that afternoon, Joselyn was still fuming mad. Sitting at her desk and staring at a blank screen, she ran the entire conversation through her mind once again. Her brain picked at every single nuance, and word said until she felt she would go crazy. This man, this perfect stranger, stormed into her world and proceeded to make assumptions, generalizations, and to treat her as if she had no restraint. Granted, he was one hot guy, and she had enjoyed a few looks and maybe a couple of wicked thoughts, but it didn't mean she had no self-control. Glancing out the window, she frowned as he slowly walked past, glaring at the ground and mumbling to himself. Turning back to the screen, she exhaled. If he didn't get his head out of his butt and soon, she would send him on his way, and the consequences be hanged. She didn't have the time or the energy to deal with his foolishness on top of deadlines, plot twists and oh yeah, that small thing called "being scared for your life."

She shook her head wearily. He was as hard and cold as the countertops in her kitchen; unyielding, but proficient as far as she could tell. She hoped this whole messy situation could be taken care of sooner rather than later, because living near him was going to drive her up a wall.

Placing her fingers on the keyboard, she took in a deep breath and let it out slowly. "Alright, Deidre, let's find some clues and get this mystery solved," she muttered.

Sometime later, the loud sound of a throat clearing snapped her head up and sent a scream from her lips. Grasping her chest, she gasped and attempted to calm her racing heart. "You scared the bejesus out of me. Haven't you ever heard of knocking?"

His lips twitched ever so slightly. "The door was open." His tone was a low rumble, and she tamped down her attraction to it and its owner. The fact he could still affect her after the dressing down he had given her irked her.

"You move like a ghost, and I'm already on edge. Give a girl a clue next time."

"Noted," he curtly replied with a chin dip before changing the subject. "We need to discuss your security issues."

Well, here it was, the moment of truth. No doubt, he was about to give her another dose of condemnation for whatever lapses there were in her present situation. Leaning back, she pointed to the chair beside her desk. "Alright, let's get this done. Have a seat, Mr. Benson."

He shook his head and clasped his hands behind his back again. "I prefer to stand, and please call me River. We are going to be spending a lot of time together so we should at least be on a first-name basis. Now, the pros - your property rests on a cul-de-sac in a gated community with limited access. The wall is solid stone, eight feet tall and capped with iron spikes. This creates a barrier that will discourage intruders from scaling it. Your property is situated back from your neighbors with a good easement between the parcels. There is an electronic alarm system in use. It's antiquated but functioning." He pursed his lips a moment gathering his thoughts. "There aren't many cons, but they will need to be addressed. The security connects via a hard line and can be severed easily. I'll need to get you a better option, possibly GSM wireless with motion detectors and off-site record storage. I would suggest installing cameras inside the dwelling as well as outside. The existing recording system is not adequate. The definition is much too low, and the camera housings are entirely too big. If someone tries to infiltrate here, they can see the cameras and avoid them. The back and side yards are too dark. We need to connect a lighting system. I'd prefer static low lights coupled with motion-sensitive halogen floods and battery backups. The bushes around your house are thick and high. They need to be either removed or trimmed to eighteen inches. Same goes for the garden on the south side of your property. Even though it's still early in the season, those vines are already heavy, and once they fill out on the pergola, it will become a blind spot. Also, the climbing roses on the trellises need to be trimmed back. The live oak tree limbs extending over the wall have to go."

"No."

The surprise on his face was comical, and she would have laughed if she hadn't been so angry. Standing slowly, she leaned forward and braced her hands on the smooth top of her desk. Taking a deep breath, she counted to five mentally and let it out. "No, River, the tree will not be cut. It is almost two hundred years old, and its existence is one of the selling points for the house. There's a reason the wall has no cap back there. It's to allow the tree limbs to grow. I'll agree to trim the bushes because they are getting a little too tall. I'll contact my lawn service in the morning. However, another hard "no" to the trumpet vines on the pergola and an "absolutely not" to the rose bushes. I had those transplanted from my parents' house in Florida. Nobody is touching them." She saw his jaw tighten as she denied his requests. Hoping to ease the sting a bit, she added, "I'll agree to a new security system; whatever you feel I need. As for security cameras inside the house, that is not happening. I don't want anyone recording me when I'm relaxing. The last thing I need is to become another viral YouTube star."

Well, that seemed to get a rise from Mr. Tall and Frosty. A line appeared between his eyes as he frowned but immediately smoothed. "I'll concede to no cameras inside. I can deal with the roses and vines if you will allow them to be trimmed back and the trellis removed. Please be reasonable concerning them. If they are clipped back now, there will be plenty of time for them to re-grow after your stalker is captured."

"No."

He scrubbed his hand over his face before changing tactics. "Those two areas are security risks. Anyone can get onto your property by utilizing those low limbs to scale the wall. The pergola and trellis create a shadowed, protected area where someone can hide with a gun. I can't protect you against irrational emotion."

She sat back down and leaned back. She would concede he had a point. However, after the way he had treated her in the coffee shop, she felt the childish need to rebel. "Douglas McClane always used a knife to kill his victims, not a gun. I'm sure putting motion detectors and lights around the garden and tree will be sufficient."

"We can start there. It's not ideal, but it's better than the alternative." He turned to go but stopped after a couple of steps.

"Is there anything else?" she asked coolly.

"Look, I think we got off on a bad footing back at the diner. I'm here to do a job."

"Yes, you said as much at the diner. Clearly."

He winced at the venom in her voice. "About that, I may have been a little harsh."

She raised her eyebrow. "A little?"

"Alright, maybe a lot," he capitulated. Flashing her a smile, he continued. "I know it's no excuse, but I'm a little tired, things are uncertain in my life right now and you... well, this whole situation took me by surprise. I swear to you I'll do everything in my power to ensure your safety. All I ask is for you to listen to my suggestions and follow my instructions. I'm not going to demean you. If I ask you to do something, there's a good reason for it. Alright?"

Twunk. His smile hit her right between her eyes,

and she widened them in shock. He had a great smile. Beautiful white teeth with a slight dimple in his right cheek. Holy cow! She wondered how she could get him to smile more.

"Ms. Kendrik? Joselyn?"

She blinked and looked at him. "Huh?"

"Are we alright?"

Joselyn closed her mouth from where his superpowered smile had scattered her thoughts. It took her a moment to comprehend his words. "Yes, we're okay," she managed to say. She understood all too well about uncertainty. Her life had been turned upside down in one way or another for years.

With a curt nod and a slight twitch of his lips he turned and strolled toward the door. "I'm going to get the ball rolling on those changes. Until then, stay inside and away from windows and doors." He hesitated. "Please?"

"Okay," she acquiesced as he disappeared. "Well, that was unexpected. The Frost Giant can thaw a bit, hmmm?" As she turned back to her computer, a thought suddenly occurred to her. If River used his smile on her often, she was going to end up with a lot of changes in her life. For some reason, those changes might not be as repulsive as they should.

Chapter 5

So much activity.

He watched as men scurried about, bringing in boxes and tools as they went about their business. Standing under the tree in the side yard of a house near his prize, he watched with a sneer as they tried to protect her. It wouldn't do any good. When the time was right, he would reach in and pluck his Little Rose right from under their noses.

As he bit into an apple, his dark gaze zeroed in on the man standing at the door talking to the security system agent. The new bodyguard would be the wild card but nothing unmanageable. The way he handled himself with that self-righteous air of superiority, he was most likely military. The observer systematically dismissed him from thought. The Army liked them big and dumb so that the new guard would be no match for cunning and ingenuity. With a toss of the core into the trash, he focused on the object of his desire as she emerged from the house. She addressed a woman pruning the shrubs then disappeared inside. Unable to stand only a glimpse of her, he withdrew a piece of paper from his pocket and stared at it. Unfolding it carefully, he gazed adoringly at the image he had captured from the internet. The page was worn and tattered in places, but the likeness to his obsession was still clear. Slowly he stroked the woman's face with an almost tender manner. Joselyn, wearing her stunning purple dress, looked so defiant and proud standing in the juror's box. Form-fitting, the dress showed off her figure perfectly by showcasing each gentle swell, dip, and flair of her nubile body. Though he couldn't see it in *this photo, he knew the sweetheart neckline revealed a hint of creamy skin along with a smattering of pale freckles. The bodice clung to her breasts, hugging her torso before flaring to her knees. The color suited her pale complexion and accentuated her long tresses. His fingers itched to stroke the sweet silk of her beautiful locks, a shimmering dark blonde. Already, he ached to taste her lips as they gasped her last breath. He could practically smell the sweet aroma of her terror as she begged and pleaded for her life. He closed his eyes as he imagined the contrast of crimson against the milky white flesh. He could picture exactly how she would appear, his greatest creation, the ultimate masterpiece. Beautiful. Exquisite. Perfection. He wanted to touch himself and get lost in the pleasure of knowing she was so close and would soon be where she belonged with him, under him, pleasing him with her whimpers and tears. He shuddered. Now was not the time to get lost in fantasies. Part of the pleasure was the stalking of his prey, and he wouldn't deny himself that. Instead, he groaned, reached down and performed a minor adjustment. He could wait; he had patience. He felt inspired and quickly pulled out a pen. Yes, she would be his. Turning the picture over, he began to write as the inky shadows swallowed him with their wraith-like arms.*

Joselyn stretched her arms over her head slowly and grimaced as joints creaked and popped. Standing, she hit the save button and yawned. She glanced over at the wall while rubbing her lower back and squinted. Already after nine pm and she was exhausted. It had been a productive day even with all the commotion casting her home into an uproar. She was almost eight thousand words closer to her goal. Apparently, a renewed feeling of security was a cure for writer's block. *Who knew?*

Turning off the lights in her study, she padded down the hall to the kitchen and poked around inside the refrigerator. With a scowl, she closed the door. How long had it been since she went shopping? From the condition of her larder, it had been a while.

"Giovanni's it is then," she muttered. Wandering through the house, she was surprised to find River sitting in the living room, bolt upright on her sofa and snoring softly. She stood there in the doorway for several moments, just watching him. She knew he had not slept much the night before and from what she had gathered from their brief discussions, none the previous night as well. She wrapped her arms around herself and backed out of the room, letting him sleep. According to her new bodyguard, years of serving in the military had made him a light sleeper. It was another thing they had in common. The Witness Protection program (or WitSec) had turned her into a fitful sleeper. Even a year later, old habits had not faded. Every creak of a limb outside, every whisper of the central system starting or stopping or the soft *chink* of the ice maker woke her no matter how tired she was. Given the number of times River had checked on her, she figured he had to be exhausted. She would leave him alone and allow him to enjoy a well-deserved rest.

Quietly, she retreated to her study and made the call to the best little Italian bistro in New Orleans. With a promise to deliver within forty-five minutes, she gave her credit card information along with a nice tip and slipped outside to wait on the porch. Sitting on a little hand-crafted bench, she found at a flea market before Christmas; she leaned back against the side of the house. She loved this neighborhood. It was quiet and the residents, friendly. Twice a year they would block off the roads and have a large party complete with grilled food, music, and games for the children.

The thought of food made her stomach growl, and she rubbed it absently. Glancing at her cell, she knew dinner wouldn't be much longer. Within five minutes of the promised forty-five, the night gate guard arrived in a golf cart.

"Hey, Ms. Kendrik. Late night hankering?"

She grinned and met him on the sidewalk. "Sam, I told you to call me Joselyn. Yes, I was working late and lost track of time." She took the items from his hands. Fishing in the bag, she pulled out a small covered bowl and handed it to him along with a package of hot breadsticks. "Gio's Chicken Alfredo with extra broccoli. Enjoy."

He smiled enormously and took the container. "You're a life savior. This sure beats the frozen dinner currently defrosting on my desk. Thank you." He placed the package on the seat next to him before tipping his hat to her. "You need anything, you let me know." He suddenly looked over Joselyn's shoulder, eyes wide. He put his golf cart into reverse and quickly drove away.

"I will. Thanks, Sam," she called after him.

"That was strange," she muttered as she turned to climb the porch steps before stopping dead in her tracks. Framed in the doorway was six feet of sexy, tousle-headed, ticked off male. The scowl directed at her would scare a hardened criminal. To the casual observer, River appeared to be relaxed, but the white-knuckled clenching of the drawn sidearm pointing to the ground said otherwise. "Ah crap," she muttered, knowing she was not going to like the conversation that was soon to come. Painting on a charming smile, she lifted the packages of food in her hands. "Dinner is served," she said in a sing-song voice.

As she stepped onto the small porch, he grabbed her arm, pushed her through the open door and slammed it. Stumbling slightly, she barely managed to retain her hold on their dinner. Setting the box on the entry table she whirled around and glared at him. "*What* is your problem?"

Red crept up his face as a vein in his forehead slowly pulsed. Narrowing his eyes, he glared at her. "What's *my* problem? Seriously? I don't know what the fu..."

She stopped him by throwing a hand up in his face. "No, sir. Nuh uh. You will not curse at me nor will you ever use that word. This is still my house and I'll not tolerate it here. Ever. If you're unable to refrain from using foul language, turn around, open the door and walk out. I mean it." She crossed her arms over her chest and glared back.

His eyes narrowed as he swallowed. Silently his lips moved in what she was sure was a count to at least ten. Taking a deep breath, River let it out slowly. "Ms. Kendrik."

Ah, the ice was back. Okay, she could handle the Frost Giant. "Yes, Mr. Benson?"

A slight grin tugged his lips at her snarky tone. Quickly he toned it down. "You're right. A man should be able to express himself without being crude. I apologize for offending you and will strive not to do it again. I can't promise I'll be able to curtail it all - after all, I'm a sailor, and we have a certain reputation to protect."

She snorted. "I'll accept that. Now, are you going to explain to me what had your panties in a twist out there on the porch?"

He narrowed his eyes at her and barked out a laugh, "Panties?" He ran a hand over his jaw. Sobering, he shook his head and tried again. "Look, I'm here for your security."

"Yes, so you've frequently mentioned."

"I'll keep mentioning it as many times as it takes. There are several things wrong with this situation." He held up his fingers one at a time as he ticked them off. "One, you should know better than to be out here in the open where anyone with a rifle and scope could take you out. Two, how do you know nobody has tampered with your food? You've already avoided one attempt at poisoning. Three, every time you open that door without letting me know you're leaving, you're taking a chance of being kidnapped. And, why did you take all these chances?" he motioned toward the boxes. "For spaghetti? I hope those meatballs are worth it."

She gasped like a fish out of water. Once again, fury roared in her, and she stuttered before getting her thoughts under control. "Mr. Benson, I live in a gated community in a fantastic neighborhood protected by locked gates and a very capable security staff. I have known these people for a lot longer than I have known you. Not only am I protected in my neighborhood, but I'm also in my own home as well. You have created a fortress for me, and I do appreciate it. However, this is still my home, and I have to live here. Notice I used the word 'live,' not exist. I refuse to give this man any more power than he already has." She dropped her hand on the food boxes beside her. "That includes ordering dinner from my favorite restaurant. Giovanni's has been in business for more than fifty years and is a cornerstone of the French Quarter. What I ordered is not spaghetti and meatballs; but rather the best eggplant parmesan you will ever put in your mouth. I wasn't sure what you liked, so I also got a pizza with all the meats. It's made from scratch and is so much better than those chain stores. When I order, I always pay ahead of time, so they don't have to bring it to my door. Sam or one of the other guards runs it down to me." She sighed and began to pace. "I can't hunker down in my house and live like a recluse. I have commitments and obligations to keep. I won't break. I won't shatter. However, I'll suffocate if you don't let me breathe. I do understand your point of view and will be more careful in the future, but please understand mine and let me live. Now that we got all the unpleasantness out of the way, how about you grab these boxes and meet me in the kitchen? I'll get some plates and something to drink. I have water, sweet tea, orange juice and a bottle of red I got as a house-warming gift from my publisher. You're in the South, so the tea is liquid sugar, just to be warned. What'll it be?"

"Water is fine for me. I'd rather not drink while on duty but help yourself." He retrieved the takeout, paused and looked down at her. Reaching out, he curled a single strand of her hair around his finger. "It's not my intention to stifle you, Joselyn but when I heard you out here talking with some stranger, I thought..." He drew his hand back and shook his head. "Please be careful." He paused and tossed a sexy grin over his shoulder on his way out of the room. "And, I don't wear panties," he said with a suggestive waggle of his eyebrows.

Whoosh.

She felt her heart speed up and her stomach clench. Was the Frost Giant thawing and was he flirting with her? Dear, sweet cheebus! She was right when she noticed how his smile could affect her. His devastating grin messed with her ability to reason. Just like the last time.

She chuckled as all the ire slowly drained away. He could be quite charming when he tried. Charming and lethal at the same time. She had no doubts whatsoever he was more than capable of keeping her safe.

As she followed him out of the entryway and into the kitchen, she watched his silent yet graceful prowling. She couldn't help but appreciate the way his muscles moved under his clothes, and she felt a familiar twinge once again. Maddox Benson was too hot for his own good, even if he was also frustrating, annoying and irritating.

It was a deadly combination for both her stalker and her own heart.

Chapter 6

*R*iver completed his rounds and returned inside by way of the back door. Walking quietly through the still house, he checked the doors and windows in every room until he was sure everything was secure. Inspecting the space was easy. Joselyn had a wonderful way of making the huge house feel homely without being cluttered. There weren't a lot of knick-knacks or extra pieces of furniture. He approved. Living in WitSec for all those years and having to be ready to go at a moment's notice tended to force a person into living a minimalistic lifestyle.

Sticking his head into the study, he smiled as he watched Joselyn concentrate on the screen, her bottom lip curled over her teeth and a slight frown between her eyebrows. He marveled once again how striking she was. Yes, Joselyn Kendrik was gorgeous, motivated, driven, and snarky as well. He loved her little outbursts of spunk and the way she called him on his crap. She was not at all like the women he was normally attracted to. If the situation were different, he would be interested in asking her out, getting to know her better. He wasn't normally a man who dated - more of a "hookup for a night or two" kind of guy instead. He watched her as she typed away. She wasn't the hookup type. No, Joselyn was one of those girls you took home to meet the family. He blew out a breath and reminded himself why he couldn't go there. Moving her from client to personal was a sure way to get one or both of them killed. Drawing back, he turned away from her door. Confident everything looked the way it should; he made his way upstairs to his room. Pushing the door until it was almost closed, he pulled the SIG Sauer P226 Mk25 out of its holster and ensured the safety was still engaged. Ejecting the magazine, he checked the breach and placed it with the gun on the table next to his bed. The Navy was starting to switch over to the Glock 19 as their official handgun when he left, but all his training was with the SIG; give him familiarity any day. He had spent enough time with this model to feel as if it were an extension of himself.

Pulling out his cell, he placed a call and sat on the edge of the bed where he could keep his eyes on the door and an ear out for anything unusual.

"River."

He should be surprised Bull knew it was him calling since he blocked his number but he wasn't. Serving together, Bull always seemed to know things he shouldn't. It was only one of many qualities that had made Bull a natural leader.

River cut right to the point. "Heard anything?"

"Nope. I've gone over the files with a fine-tooth comb. The only thing I'm sure of is Douglas Beecher McClane's death. Whoever is after Ms. Kendrik, it's not him."

River nodded as if Bull could see him. "We already knew who it wasn't. We need to find out who it is."

A long drawn breath sounded over the line. "I'm trying, but I'm not even supposed to be working on this case. If I can even call it a case. As far as official channels go, it's a nuisance report at best. I'm having to work things quietly to keep my ass from getting ground up for dog food. How is she doing?"

River laughed. "Better than I am, I think. Remember the week in Costa Rica? The anticipation here is worse. It's like I'm holding my breath, waiting for something to happen."

"Maybe you being there has scared her stalker off. Look, man, I know you have things to do. You came out here at my request. If you think it's over, go ahead and go. You have security measures in place now. She'll be alright."

"Mr. Benson? River?"

He heard her call to him from the lower level. "My gut tells me this thing isn't over. I don't know who this yokel is and I don't know what he has planned. Everything in me is saying Joselyn is still in danger and I'm not going to leave her vulnerable. I got nothing better to do right now. Keep on digging. Give me something, anything. I'll check in with you in a few days."

He disconnected the call, picked up his gun, reinserted the magazine and secured it to his belt holster. He met her on the stairs. "Yes, Ma'am?"

She looked at him from the bottom of the stairs with those huge brown eyes, and he felt a hitch in his stomach. So pretty. So vulnerable. So perfect.

Don't get involved.

"We've been cooped up in this house for a while now. Don't you think it's time we dropped the formalities? Please, call me Joselyn or even Jos."

"Joselyn it is. So Joselyn, what can I do for you?"

She peered at him through the balusters. "I finished my manuscript and sent it off to the editor, so it's time to celebrate. Go put on your dress holster, shine your best combat boots and break out the formal tee-shirt because we're going to get a real dinner in a real restaurant. Somewhere other than Giovanni's. I feel like I'm one meal away from becoming a cannoli."

He couldn't help chuckling; she was so cute and feisty. Once again, it was clear to him how perfect she would be for him. He could almost imagine how perfectly she would fit tucked under his arm as they walked the streets and alleys of the French Quarter. Despite what he had told her during their first meeting, he did want to find out her hopes and dreams. He could easily see himself spending hours getting to know her. Unfortunately, he couldn't. Letting the grin fade, he forced his mind back to the business at hand. "I don't think that's a good idea, Joselyn."

She raised one eyebrow. "I always celebrate the end of a manuscript by going out to eat. After weeks of hunching over a keyboard, barely sleeping and sustaining on takeout or whatever I can scrounge from the kitchen, I need to get out. I need to associate with people who don't originate in my mind. When the story takes me, I do well to remember about showering and brushing my teeth. I forget everything else until I get it's done. Nope, we are going out. I'm going to get ready, and I'll meet you in the living room in a half hour. With or without you, Maddox, I'm blowing this popsicle stand for a while." She smirked mischievously. "I'll even let you drive me, so you don't have to fold yourself up into my car. See, I can be reasonable." She climbed the stairs. "I'm in the mood for something authentic like gumbo and crawfish etouffee." She bumped against his hip on her way by and disappeared into her room.

He watched the door close and heard the shower start in her bathroom. Immediately visions of how she would look naked with water sluicing over her body danced through his head and filled his body with want. Shoving it down, he muttered to himself, "You're only interested in her safety. Nothing else, SEAL. Keep it in your pants."

He knew it for the lie it was and snorted.

"So there I was, sitting at my first convention with stacks of books, a handful of markers and no idea what to do. I felt a hand on my shoulder, and it startled me. I jumped. Books and pens flew everywhere. Immediately I got down on the floor and started to gather everything together before it could get stomped on. I glanced up, and Annabeth was looking at me with a quizzical expression. Next to her was a tall man with long black hair, blue eyes and covered in tattoos. She leans toward him slowly and says in a conspiratorial whisper, 'It's the medications. I promise we'll fix the dosage before the next book comes out.' Then she introduced me to Martin Strong, two-time Male Romance Model of the Year and the cover for my next novel. I was completely mortified to meet both him and my literary agent for the first time while scrambling around on my knees."

Laughing, talking, and simply existing was easy. Each moment he spent with Joselyn hammered the point home. She was funny, sweet, beautiful and he loved spending time with her. She was also pretty smart, and though River hated to admit it, she had been right. They both needed a little R&R. It was nice to get away and almost forget. He motioned to the waiter. "Check, please," he said before he turned his attention back to her.

"In my second book, Deidre teamed up with a Marine to solve the crime. I did a lot of research, so I know you military guys give each other nicknames for some pretty strange reasons at times. So where did 'River' come from?" Joselyn drained the last of the wine from her glass and leaned forward, resting her chin on her hands.

The waiter returned with the check, and she lunged to grab it, but River pulled it away. "Nuh-uh, this one's on me." He pulled out a card and dropped it on top of the leather guest check sleeve after glancing at the total.

"Why, Mr. Benson, how positively gallant," she gushed in a faux Southern belle accent. She batted her eyelashes at him. "But don't get into the habit of paying. Speaking of, we haven't discussed what I'm paying you for your help. I guess we should have talked about it before now." Her face fell. "Crapadoo, can I even afford you?"

He threw his head back and laughed. "You can afford me since I'm doing this for free. I owed Bull a favor, and he called it in. "

"I can't allow you to do that. I have to pay you something. Your time is valuable."

"I said don't worry about it."

"Easy for you to say," she retorted. "I want to pay you for your expertise at least."

"Uncle Sam already did. Joselyn, don't sweat it; I'm glad to help out. To be honest, it's giving me a little break before I have to decide what I'm going to do with the rest of my life. Who knows, maybe I'll go into professional bodyguarding after this and I have you to thank for it."

She snorted. "Or you'll run screaming when you realize how bad it can be."

He laughed again. "You have a wonderful sense of humor."

"Thank you, but don't think I've forgotten what we were talking about. Seriously, how did you get your nickname?"

"No chance of letting that go, eh? Since you insist on knowing, it was during BUD/s."

She sat up straight. "You're a SEAL?"

"Well done. Most civilians don't know what that means." He drained the last of his water, signed the ticket after adding a good tip and replaced his card in his wallet. "Fourteen years."

Her mouth dropped open as her eyes widened. "I knew you were in the military from what Detective Jameson said, but I didn't know you were in special forces. Wow, I'm impressed."

He shrugged. "It's not something we advertise." He leaned back and rested his hands on his stomach. "Back to your question; it was the first week of BUD/s. We were all sitting around, shooting the breeze and the subject of nicknames came up. Already, a couple had earned a new moniker, but I knew enough to keep my head down and my mouth shut. The last thing I wanted was to be saddled with a name that was just a big joke. The one they decided on wasn't too bad to be honest, as it could have been a lot worse. You see, most of the guys entered the program right out of training, but I had already been in for six years. I was the old man in the group. There's one guy, Hick, who asked me why I didn't already have one. I said I was too old to worry about nicknames, but that excuse didn't go over too well." He chuckled at the memory. "Hick snapped his fingers and said, 'You're from Mississippi, and you're the old man here. Old Man River.'" He shrugged, "And there it is."

Joselyn studied him for a moment. He could feel her eyes sweep his features. He wanted to crow with pride because she seemed to like whatever it was she saw in him. Finally, she spoke. "I think it's a great name for you. Rivers are calm on the surface but underneath deadly and dangerous. They are a force to be reckoned with and given the right circumstances and time, can make changes in their environment. Yeah, I think they gave you the ideal name. From what I've seen, it fits you perfectly."

"Why, Ms. Kendrik, how positively gallant," he quipped.

They sat there in silence, gazing at each other until finally she cleared her throat and blushed. "It's getting late," she muttered as she stood and swayed slightly. Perhaps it was the moment or the ridiculous heels she wore, but River was pretty sure it had more to do with the bottle she had consumed. Immediately, he shot to his feet and pulled her securely against his body. She felt right, pressed against him, all soft and curves. He couldn't help himself; he laid his head on hers, closed his eyes and inhaled her scent. She smelled amazing - like orange blossoms and the Chianti still sitting on the table. He stroked his hand up her back and underneath her hair, touching the warm skin with his fingertips. A part of him knew they couldn't be more, that he couldn't go any further than this moment, so he committed it to his memory. It would have to be enough when this was over, and he went on to whatever his life would become. Suddenly, only memories of Joselyn didn't feel like enough and yet it would have to be. He sighed and gently pushed her back.

She looked up at him with misunderstanding. "I don't," she started.

He hated the betrayal glimmering in her eyes. "It's better this way," he murmured away. Motioning for her to precede him, River followed her out of the restaurant, careful to keep his eyes on the other guests, the floor, the wall, the door - anywhere but Joselyn.

Reaching the parking lot, she suddenly stopped and gasped. Immediately, he went on point, pulling his weapon and looking for danger. Not seeing anything, he pointed the handgun toward the concrete and closed the distance to her. "What is it," he whispered.

He searched her face. She was pale, and her eyes were wide. Instead of answering, she pointed with one trembling finger toward his truck. Fluttering on the hood was a piece of paper with a small jar sitting on top. Taking the last few steps, he stood in front of his Ford. He read the words on the paper.

Busy little bees working the hive,
Struggling to keep their queen alive.
Drones attend to obtain favor,
Workers to toil in their tiresome labor.
A soldier guards the queen at home,
But cannot stop the end to come.
Poor little queen, sealed by fate,
The soldier's attempts will be too late.

Inside the jar, floating in what was most likely honey, were several bees. They were all intact except for one; the largest had been decapitated. Back on the farm in Mississippi, River's aunt and uncle had once possessed several beehives to harvest honey. He knew without a shadow of a doubt the decapitated one was a queen. Fury like he had never felt before swept over him. The bastard was still out there, still hunting her. He was obviously aware of who River was, as well as the part he played in all this. A growl erupted from his throat as he glared at the empty lot, searching for the culprit. There was no one around. Placing his sidearm into its holster once again, he cradled Joselyn next to his body and hurried her back to the restaurant. Once he had her sitting at the hostess station and was sure she was okay, he withdrew his cell and pushed a number. When it connected, he snarled into the device.

"Bull, meet me at the parking lot on Iberville near Royal. There's another gift."

Chapter 7

The silence felt heavy and oppressive as they silently rode to Joselyn's house. Glancing over, she studied River's face as he drove, both hands gripping the steering wheel with white knuckles. Once Detective Jameson had arrived with a crime scene team, River had shut her out. The Frost Giant was back.

Joselyn tried so hard to be brave, but the weight of this situation was crippling her. It was the program all over. Once again, her life was not her own. As before, she had to keep one eye trained behind her at all times and every action she took must be scrutinized and evaluated. Drawing a breath, she let it out carefully, willing her heart to slow from its frantic drumming in her chest. Douglas Beecher McClane was stalking her. She knew he was supposed to be deceased. She knew Maddox, Detective Jameson and everyone in the free world thought he was dead but she knew better. The person causing all this anxiety was not some random stalker copycat. She knew it was ludicrous to believe he was still alive but she couldn't shake the feeling. Something inside her told her it was him.

"You're not crazy."

She looked over at River. "What?"

"I said you aren't crazy. I know you feel like

everyone thinks you are, but you aren't."

She gave out a choked laugh. "Yeah sure."

He reached over and clasped her hand in his. Gently, he squeezed it. "I mean it. You have been through a lot. Douglas McClane took your security, your freedom, and your confidence. For three years, his actions ruled yours. Now, this guy comes along and does the same again. It's the same actions, the same feelings, the same inability to do what you want. It's natural for you to feel this way. Being scared isn't being crazy. In this situation, it's smart." He pulled up to the gate and stopped. Entering his code, he drove through, waving to Sam at the gate and pulled into her driveway. Once the truck was parked, he continued. "Joselyn, I swear to you. No matter who this man is, McClane, or a copycat or some sick fu... creep who gets his jollies trying to scare you; I'm not going to let anything happen to you. Do you hear what I'm saying? Nothing is going to happen to you. If one good thing came out of tonight, Bull is now opening a full case for you that he can actively work. He is smart, wily, and has instincts off the chart. He's going to figure out who is doing this to you. Until he does, I'll be right here, watching your six, keeping you safe. You have two SEALs working to take care of this for you, Okay?"

She nodded but wouldn't meet his gaze. Sure, a part of her knew it was impossible for her stalker to be McClane but it was a small part. This terror felt the same. It felt like those three years hiding in safe houses, looking over her shoulder and waiting for the moment he would finally get to her. It was insane, absurd. She had seen the report, and the pictures of the man stretched out and faced up on the cemetery lawn. He had the same chin and lips and the same hair, although drenched in blood. Except for the bullet holes on his forehead and cheek which destroyed his face on one side, it was the same. There was no question it was Douglas McClane. He. Was. Dead. If she knew it, why couldn't she trust herself?

"Come on. I think it's time to break into that bottle of red sitting in your fridge." River got out of the truck, scanned the area before going to her side. Opening the door, he helped her out of the truck and ushered her toward the door in front of him. Shielding her from the open, they went inside, disarmed the alarm and locked it behind.

"Stay here," he murmured as he pulled his weapon and quickly made a sweep of the house. It was obvious nobody had entered since the alarm had not sounded, but she was glad he was checking anyway. It made her feel... safer.

Several minutes passed before he returned to the entryway. "All clear." He led her into the den and seated her in front of the fireplace. Within minutes, he had a nice fire going. He pulled an afghan from the sofa and placed around her shoulders. "I'll get you a glass of wine."

She watched him leave and felt something in her twist. He was so protective and strong. It wasn't fair she couldn't be strong as well. She thought she had possessed a decent grip on things. Up until the moment she discovered the latest gift, she was sure she could handle anything. She hated what she had become - a weak, uncertain, frightened version of herself. Now she felt like a piece of dandelion fluff caught in a windstorm. Her stalker, McClane or copycat, had proven he could get to her when he was ready. Instantly, she understood hopelessness. Before, while still in WitSec, she hadn't received any gifts or creepy poems, and though frightened she understood she was safe. Now, knowing he could reach out and pluck her like the rose he called her, terrified her. She tasted salt and realized the tears threatening to fall had finally made their way down her face. She heard River return and quickly wiped her cheeks with the corner of the cover. He handed her a glass half full of the deep red wine. She smiled but couldn't meet his eyes.

He muttered a curse, and she didn't even chastise him. Did she trust River to keep her safe? She wasn't sure. She didn't trust anyone right now. Taking a sip of the vintage, she frowned. It tasted like ashes in her mouth. Placing the glass on the table, she pulled herself to her feet. "I'm going to go to bed," she mumbled before walking woodenly to the stairs. Tomorrow she would get herself together, but for tonight, all she wanted was to sleep.

No, that's not exactly true. What she *really* wanted was to feel River's arms around her and to hear his whispered assurances saying she wouldn't come to harm. She knew he was Special Forces. She knew it was wrong to feel this way about him. She knew nothing would ever come of her romantic notions concerning him. Yes, she knew all of this but her heart wasn't listening. Right now, she needed his strength, his care. She needed him, but it was not to be. He made it very clear every chance he could.

Changing into her pajamas, Joselyn slid into bed.

Curling on her side, she closed her eyes, but instead of the dark, she saw Douglas McClane's face as he screamed at her in the courtroom. She shuddered and bit her lip to keep a sob from erupting. Her heart raced in her chest, and sweat poured down her back. Fighting to maintain control, she chastised herself. She didn't want River to see her fall apart. She heard him climb the stairs and stop outside her door. Holding her breath, she waited until he entered his room. Then and only then, would she allow the tears to fall.

She closed her eyes and pulled her favorite comforter up over her head. Staring into the blackness, the words with his revolting gift flickered through her mind over and over. When sleep finally claimed her, it was only after her pillow was thoroughly soaked and exhaustion forced her into the arms of her nightmares.

He couldn't sleep.

Lying on the bed down the hall from Joselyn, River stared at the red glowing numbers of the clock on the table. When the digital numbers read 4:30, he threw the cover off. He might as well get up. There wasn't going to be any more sleep tonight.

Rising swiftly, he grabbed a tee-shirt out of the drawer and tugged it on along with a ratty pair of shorts. Sliding his feet into his gym shoes, he checked his SIG and strapped it into an underarm holster. Sliding a small knife into a sheath strapped to his ankle, he stood and stretched. Quickly he swept the house again before exiting the front door. Putting in the code, he slipped out and waited for the faint acceptance of the rearming chime. Turning his face toward the second floor of darkened windows, he felt a clench in his belly. He hated to leave her, even for a few minutes but he had to do this. Normally, he used the treadmill in Joselyn's little basement home gym to get his daily five-mile run. Today, it wouldn't be enough. He needed to check the neighborhood. He convinced himself it was diligent, but he knew it was because of the way she had melted last night. He had to do something, and he needed to clear his head.

Doing a couple of stretches to loosen his muscles, he jogged to the road, turned left and out into the neighborhood. With a chin lift, he acknowledged Sam in the guardhouse as he passed. The guard waved then went back to watching something on a small laptop. River frowned. He knew it was allowed by Joselyn's HOA, but he didn't like it. He much rather the guards pays closer attention even if they were mostly non-essential.

Immediately, his thoughts turned toward Joselyn. She was beautiful, feisty and so strong. Until last night, he would have thought nothing could shake her, but now he knew better. He couldn't get the haunted look in her eyes out of his mind. One minute she had been happy, laughing and joking with him at dinner and the next, it was all she could do to not fall to pieces. He hated seeing her that way. She had an undeniable spark which made him sometimes wonder if she truly needed him. Not that he didn't think she was in danger. No, the toxicology report on those strawberries assured him she did need help. The events last night solidified it. However, until they found her new gift, she seemed unshakeable. The note and honey left on his truck had shattered her. He grimaced as he recalled the blood draining from her face and her body trembling as he held her against him. Last night hadn't only scared her; it had terrified her.

Rounding a corner, he disappeared into the next cul-de-sac, following the road. The neighborhood was quiet. She had chosen well in making a home here. With a few tweaks, he had made sure she was as secure as she could be. Pushing himself to go a bit faster, he noted absently how this area was not as well lit as Joselyns. He looked up to see the street lamp out. Glancing down quickly, he didn't see any glass littering the roadside, so it was probably a few days old. He made a mental note to let Sam know when he returned to the main gate.

Returning his thoughts to her, he began to categorize what he knew about her stalker mentally. Other than an obvious fascination with both Joselyn and the 'The Gardener,' they didn't have much to go on. Maybe he should contact her former handler in WitSec to get his spin on things. He nodded to himself. Yeah, that would be a great place to start.

Reaching the final road leading to the smaller, unmanned, secondary gate, he continued down and around. The first night here, he had run this same route, familiarizing himself with her neighborhood. The houses in this section were the newest and backed up against a high, stone privacy wall. A park spread out beyond it. Cutting across the yard of an empty house for sale, he reached the wall and pushed himself to the top. The wall itself was about a foot wide and had tall metal poles topped with lights. Looking over the edge, he noted someone would have to have a ladder to breach this barrier as the ground dropped away a good twelve feet to the manicured playground below. He glanced up the length of the wall and noticed a gate atop a set of gently curving rock steps with a digital pad for residents to use if they wanted to escape into the area. He nodded. The gate, like the other two, had bars too close together to let anything other than a small animal through. Satisfied all was as it should be, he jumped lightly from the wall and retraced his steps back.

By the time he saw the guardhouse again, a fine sweat had covered his body. Stopping to tell Sam about the lamp, he retreated to Joselyn's house. A sense of relief washed over him as he stepped onto her drive. The run had only been about two miles, but he didn't feel like leaving her again. He had needed to check the neighborhood to ensure himself everything was okay. Now he would complete his exercise on the treadmill in her house.

Letting himself in, he reset the code. Quickly, he checked all the rooms, doors and windows. Nothing seemed out of the ordinary. Stopping at his room, he removed the knife and sheath but kept the SIG with him. Hesitating briefly at the doorway of Joselyn's room, he watched her sleep for a few minutes. He frowned as she tossed and turned, making little sounds of distress. Maybe he should wake her? He took a step into her room then stopped. He recalled too well how she felt in his arms last night - tiny, afraid, trembling. The haunting fear in her eyes tore a hole in his gut. He was in deep, and he knew it. He wanted her. There, he said it. He wanted her with everything in his soul. It was too easy to imagine holding her, comforting her, being with her. She would make him happy, just by letting him be a part of her world. However, there were so many reasons why he couldn't, and the biggest one was crystal clear. She was his client. He shook his head and retreated from her room.

His client.

Making his way to the basement, he set the machine and stepped on. Gradually he increased the tempo until it was at a fast run. He ran as hard as he could, punishing his body for thinking about her like that. He had no right to her. He was here to watch over her and to keep some schmuck from getting his hands on her. There could be nothing more. Once she was safe, she would go back to her life, and he would try to find where he fit into his world, post SEALs. After fifteen minutes running at such a grueling pace, he hopped off. Gasping hard, he sucked in oxygen as fast as his aching lungs allowed. Snatching a towel, he wiped the sweat from his drenched face and threw it against the wall with a curse. Bending over, he braced his hands on his knees and closed his eyes. He couldn't run away from the truth. He had tried to distance himself, but he was tired of fighting it.

Joselyn was his to protect.

His to care for.

His.

Chapter 8

*T*oday was going to suck.

Joselyn checked her reflection in the mirror and sighed wearily. The little bit of sleep she'd gotten had been full of menacing dreams and outright nightmares. Her face told the story. Dark circles sat heavily under her eyes, and worry lines were showing between her carefully arched brows. She searched through her makeup until she found a tube of concealer and applied it liberally to the area until the darkness lightened to a manageable level. A few drops of eyewash and she was ready to go.

She checked her forest green sweater and dark wash jeans in the mirror. A smile flittered across her face. Paired with her favorite boots, she gave off an air of approachable perfection. She wanted her fans to be unafraid of talking to her. Pulling her hair back with a black and green headband, she checked herself again and nodded. "Ready or not, here I go," she muttered as she reminded herself book signings were a favorite part of this new career.

Grabbing bags full of swag she would give out, she made her way downstairs. River was waiting by the door. His eyes widened, and he gave her one of those slow grins that heated her. "Wow. You look great."

She blushed. "Thank you." Her eyes slid over his body, and she had to admit to herself that River looked pretty awesome himself. Wearing an eye matching blue dress shirt with sleeves rolled to mid-arm, and dark slacks, he pulled off the casual look perfectly. His ever-present gun sat prominently on his right hip in what he called, 'a quick release holster.' Normally she was not a gun enthusiast, but on him, it looked dangerous but capable. She dragged her sight from his hips upward to his face. He had shaved this morning, leaving the ghost of a beard and his deep black hair was just a little shaggy. Not for the first time, she wondered about his hair length. She had always assumed military men wore their hair 'high and tight,' but River's brushed his collar. Shaking herself, she cleared her throat. She could gather wool over her sexy bodyguard some other time. "I'm ready. The books should be waiting there, and I have the gifts here."

He took two steps and gently pulled the bags from her hands. "I'll get this," he murmured.

She let him pull them from her fingers, but he didn't move. Instead, he stared at her, his eyes slowly taking in her features. She swallowed under the heat of his perusal until she couldn't keep his gaze any longer. She wanted to reach out and touch his face, to cup his cheek in her palm and feel the rough scruff of his jaw. She wanted to touch her lips to his and see if he tasted as exotic as she thought. She wanted to feel his arms around her again and to get lost in his quiet strength. She wanted so much, and none of it was for her. He had made it abundantly clear. She forced herself to turn and walk toward the door. It wouldn't do any good for her to wish and want when she couldn't have what she needed.

During her study of him, she swore something had changed between last night and now. She wasn't sure exactly what it was, but it confused her. When she went to bed last night, broken and frightened, he had been so distant. Now? She shook her head. He seemed softer, somehow. No, not soft exactly. Maybe the appropriate word would be *accessible*. She sighed. Glancing over her shoulder, she saw him studying her with an unreadable expression. There was heat there and something almost tender in the way he watched her. Knowing there was a stalker out there waiting for her, she should feel afraid; instead, she felt precious and important. Even cared for.

Pushing it from her mind, she fixed a bright smile on her face. "You ready? I hate to be late, and we don't know what the traffic will be like."

He drew in a breath and let it go. "Joselyn, I really don't like you going to this."

She laughed. "I know. You've told me this for the past four hours. Book signings are important, and I can't blow it off. You talked to the security guard at the bookstore, and you'll be right there glaring at anyone who gets close to me. I'll be fine." She rested her palm on his arm but pulled away when tingles shot through her arm from the brief contact.

If he felt the shock, he didn't let on. Instead, he motioned her ahead and followed her. She watched as he locked the door and listened for the chirp signaling the alarm was armed. Together, they went to his truck. She slid into the passenger side as he piled the bags in the back seat. Within minutes, they were on their way through the suburbs of New Orleans. He flipped the radio on, and she couldn't help but smile as he hummed along with the song on the radio, tapping his fingers on the steering wheel. Moments like this she could almost pretend they were two ordinary people, out together on a date without a care in the world. Relaxing against the leather seat, she watched him. Rugged, handsome and protective - all were perfect adjectives to describe him. Suddenly, he looked over at her and flashed her a beautiful smile. Her heart hitched in her chest as she answered his smile with one of her own. When he was at ease and comfortable, he was so darn gorgeous he took her breath away. Reaching over, she dared to touch his leg. He tensed but relaxed. Yes, for a moment, they could pretend they were normal. After the craziness of her life lately, normal sounded pretty great to her. The moment ended when he pulled into the parking lot of the giant bookstore. As soon as the truck stopped, the ease lifted and the Frost Giant was back. She understood the reasoning, but she mourned the loss.

For the next two hours, she signed books, talked to her fans and took copious amounts of pictures with them. Throughout it all, River stood behind her, arms crossed and a permanent scowl on his face. Glancing over her shoulder, she saw him scan the crowded room, and she knew he wasn't happy. She shrugged. He would have to get over it.

"Ms. Chambers, is he a model for the next book cover? He looks exactly how I imagined John Michaels to be. Deidre's boyfriend is so hot and yummy!"

Joselyn was taking a drink of water and almost

choked. Coughing she wiped her watering eyes and shook her head. "No, he's not a cover model." She grinned mischievously. "He's hot enough to be one though isn't he?" She winked at the forty-something woman who sighed dreamily as she gazed at him. With a chuckle, Joselyn signed the book and handed it back to her. Behind her, River snorted.

The line snaking through the store and out the door slowly dwindled to nothing. Finally, she was able to stretch her back. Now she could take a few minutes and confirm a few emails, including one sent by the store owner for another signing in a few weeks. Opening her purse, she searched for her cell phone and growled. Where was it?

"You okay?" River asked her low.

"I can't find my cell phone. "

He frowned. "Where was the last place you had it?"

She thought for a moment. "Last night at the restaurant. We were trying to remember who starred in that movie and I looked it up." She dug through her purse again. "Great, just great. I have my notes, all my contacts. Oh God, the pictures of my dad." She started to panic and rifled through her purse again.

"Maybe you took it out and put it on the charger?"

She shook her head. "No, I left my purse on the table by the door. I didn't touch it until we left to come here. I haven't even opened my purse until now. It was still zipped. "

He squeezed her shoulder. "Calm down. I'll check in the truck. You probably dropped it. Stay here. I'll be right back."

He jogged out the door.

Joselyn placed her purse back on the floor under the table and smiled at the next person in line. "Hi. How would you like this?"

She signed the book along with the next two before River returned. "I looked all through the truck; it's not there, so I called the restaurant. They checked around and even had someone run out to the parking lot. I'm sorry."

She sighed and forced a smile. "It's okay. It was an old one anyway and past time to upgrade. I hope it backed up recently."

He looked a little upset but gave a quick chin drop. "It's ten to three now. You're almost done. I'll feel better once we are out of here."

"Okay," she whispered before she greeted the next person. Taking the proffered novel, she smiled at the owner and hastily scribbled on the title page.

Suddenly, from behind, she heard a quick intake of breath which made the tiny hairs on her arms rise. Joselyn glanced over her shoulder and saw River tense, his eyes narrowed to the right. Following his gaze, she saw a slight man dressed in black with a hoodie pulled low over his brow and wearing dark sunglasses. He was staring at her, and she felt chills race down her back. "River," she murmured with a tiny hitch in her voice.

"I see him," he replied and took off at a brisk stride.

She sat still, pen in one hand and book opened to the title page in the other. She held her breath as River reached the man and spun him around, pushing him against a wall and spilling a display of DIY books. Joselyn sprang to her feet and covered her mouth with both hands. Was this her stalker? Hurrying over, she stood close by as the entire store silenced and people gawked at the intense scene unfolding.

"Who are you and what do you want with my woman, I mean Joselyn... er... Ms. Kendrik. Why are you here bothering Ms. Kendrik?"

Joselyn's eyebrows disappeared in her hairline as a flock of butterflies took up residence in her belly. He had said, "my woman" before catching himself. "What do you mean?" she asked in a confused tone.

He flinched and shot her a look over his shoulder. With the hint of a shake, he conveyed to her his desire to not talk about it. She would acquiesce. For now. He gave her a grateful wink and turned his attention to the man shoved against the wall.

A funny kind of warmth spread through her body and the butterflies became hummingbirds. He'd called her *his woman*. She felt almost giddy at the words. To some, it may seem chauvinistic, but she didn't care. He had claimed her, albeit unconsciously. Maybe he *did* feel the same way as her after all. She wanted to shout and twirl in circles. *His woman*. She knew there was probably a stupid grin on her face, but she just couldn't bring herself to care. He'd called her his and no matter what, nothing could take that from her now.

Her attention strayed back to them as Maddox shook the man again. "Answer me. Why are you watching Joselyn?"

Around them, people were whispering, and more than a few cell phones were out and recording. She groaned. This had YouTube written all over it.

The man swallowed and struggled. "Please, let me go," he whined.

The security guard pushed his way through the crowd and tried to pull River off the smaller one. He would have had more luck pulling a train off a track. "Hey now, don't be harassing the customers," he warned.

River ignored him. "I asked you who you are and why you're staring at Joselyn."

A tiny sound left his lips like a squeak. "I'm a huge fan. I... I... I was trying to get the nerve to ask for her autograph."

The words sounded strange; almost high pitched. River must have come to the same conclusion. He pulled the hood down and knocked the sunglasses off his face.

It wasn't a man but rather a woman. Slight in stature with short mousey brown hair and big green eyes, she was even shorter than Joselyn and couldn't be more than nineteen or twenty. Realizing his mistake, River let her go with a muttered curse and an apology. Retrieving her warped sunglasses from the floor, he handed them back to her. She rubbed her arm and glared at him. Snatching the glasses from his hand, she thrust them into her pocket.

"Oh gracious, I'm so sorry." Joselyn advanced, but River held her back. She glared at him. "She's a fan. You can't be manhandling them." Pushing past him, she placed a hand on the woman's shoulder. "Are you okay?"

The woman nodded then her mouth made a perfect "O." "You're... you're... Oh, my Gosh. I can't believe." The girl gushed. "I've read your books and all the short stories. I've friended you on Facebook and Instagram, and I follow you on Twitter. You're the most amazing person ever."

Joselyn blushed. "What's your name?"

"Sasha. Sasha Bruins. I... could you... I mean, is it okay?" She stooped, recovered three books and looked at Joselyn expectantly. "I was afraid I would miss you. I came all the way from Memphis to see you. Traffic was bad, but parking here is horrible. I had to park three blocks over. I just knew I was going to miss you." She glanced at Maddox and swallowed. "Are you sure it's alright?"

"Of course Sasha, come over here and we'll get you all fixed up. I promise he won't bite."

Sasha glanced at Maddox again but followed Joselyn back to her table. Joselyn spent several minutes with the girl, talking and taking pictures. She even dug out a few swag items which make Sasha almost cry. She laughed when Sasha posted the pictures on social media with the hashtags *#joselynrocks, #squeallikeafangirl, #thisjusthappened* and *#theDeidrefiles*. She would never forget the girl's face when Joselyn leaned in and whispered a couple of spoilers for the new book currently residing with her editor. By the time Sasha left with her treasures, Joselyn was smiling again and had even forgiven River for tackling the girl. Joselyn wanted to make a note to add a character named Sasha to a future novel but stopped when she remembered her cell phone was missing. Pulling out a piece of paper, she jotted down a few notes and shoved it into her satchel. Hopefully, she would find it again soon.

With the event finished, they gathered her materials and with a wave to the owner, exited the store. River piled what was left of her stuff into the back seat, got in and started the engine. Glancing over at her, he spoke.

"I'm sorry about your cell phone."

"Me too. It's my lifeline. I hadn't upgraded in the past three years because I didn't want to have to move everything. There's contacts, story plots, appointments, book ideas, not to mention pictures I would cry over if I lost. Supposedly, everything was backed up to a cloud, but I never feel overly confident in that technology."

"I can understand." He closed his eyes for a minute. Making a decision, he blew out a breath. "Everything in me is screaming to get you home where I can keep you safe, but I think for your ease of mind we should go ahead get you a new one. The sooner you feel comfortable, the better."

She felt a wave of gratitude wash over her. After the incident with Sasha, she knew too well how on edge he was. She wasn't going to ask to go but since he offered? "Yes, I would like that. Thank you, River." She reached over and squeezed his arm. "I don't think I've said it enough. Thank you for your service to our country and thank you for your help now. You have done so much to keep me safe, and I appreciate it deeply."

The ice blue of his eyes warmed, and he gave her a genuine smile. Covering her hand with his, he laced their fingers together and pulled out of the parking place. "No place I'd rather be," he stated simply as if it were only too obvious.

Looking at his fingers tangled with hers, she felt the hummingbirds turn to swans. They still needed to talk about what he meant by calling her his, but it could wait. Right now, she wanted to bask in the moment and the warmth of his hand in her lap. Even if nothing else came of it, she would carry this memory with her for a lifetime.

She sighed.

Best. Day. Ever.

Chapter 9

*R*iver's nerves were frayed. Gritting his teeth, he planted his feet and stood stoically beside Joselyn trying to keep her from getting knocked over in the small, lavish electronics store. People pushed against them time and time again. He wondered why they didn't order online. In front of him, Joselyn's attention was on a display of different cases for the latest models. An elbow caught him in the back, and he grimaced. Gritting his teeth, he barely held back a snarl as a woman muttered a hasty "Excuse me."

"So, what do you think, River?"

He turned his attention back to Joselyn. Raising an eyebrow, he asked, "What do I think about what?"

She huffed and waved three different cases. "These. Which one do you like?"

He wrinkled his brow and glanced at the boxes in her hand. "Ahh..." He swallowed and looked at her face. She watched him as he hemmed and hawed. "Honestly, they are all the same to me."

"Well, which one would you choose for yourself."

He laughed. "These are all sparkly, flowery and glittery! I wouldn't choose any of them for myself."

She chuckled and nodded. "Yeah, I guess you wouldn't, and I'm not sure I like them either. I'm more of a clear, no-frills kind of gal. I thought if I picked one that was bright, maybe I wouldn't leave it again. I still can't believe I lost mine. Normally I take better care of my things." She turned her attention back to the three boxes in her hand and chewed her bottom lip.

No frills? Yeah, it sounded about right. Joselyn was not one to call attention to herself. Maybe it had something to do with all those years she spent in hiding, but he felt it probably was also her beautiful character shining through. He remembered how she had been with Sasha in the store. Joselyn had been caring, understanding, and giving. Yes, those three words all described this woman. He flinched when he thought about his little faux pas. *His woman.* He hadn't meant to say it out loud. He hoped she had forgotten about it, but something told him she never forgot anything. There was going to be one extremely uncomfortable talk later. He glanced at her as she gnawed on her lip. Reaching over, he gently brushed his thumb over it, nudging it from the grip of her teeth. It was swollen and pink. Fire shot through his body as he imagined taking it into his mouth to taste. He wanted to suck and tease, run his tongue over and between until neither of them had breath left. So beautiful. So amazing. He groaned as she licked it and raised her eyes to him. His heart lurched and raced. So much faith with a touch of fear swam in the caramel colored depths. No matter how afraid she was, she trusted him to keep her safe. He wanted to puff out his chest in pride. He was taking care of her, keeping her safe and she knew, without a doubt, she was secure.

The moment was lost as they were jostled again.

He bit back a growl and pulled her tightly against his side. This was insane! The push of the crowd reminded River how unprotected Joselyn was and his patience was running out. When he had enough and was about to grab his charge and march out of the store, a young woman dressed in the store's distinctive gear approached them. Touching the tablet in her hands, she flashed them a smile.

"Hi. I'm Clarisse. How may I help you today."

Immediately, Joselyn warmed to the woman and explained her old telephone had been lost and she needed a new one. Flashing her a million watt smile, Clarisse motioned for them to follow her to one of the quieter kiosks in the back where additional sales people were helping other customers. "We can get you all set, no problem," she assured them before launching into a spiel about the different models of cell phones and features of each. River listened half-heartedly to the two discuss things as he continued to scan the area. He was paranoid. Joselyn was safe. Nobody would dare to attempt hurting her with a hundred people nearby. He felt a little of the tension drain away.

"And what do you think, Mr. Kendrik?"

River's attention drew back to Clarisse, and he frowned. "I'm sorry what?"

Joselyn gave out a half laugh as her cheeks flushed. "Oh, he's not my husband," she assured the woman. "He's... ah..."

River chuckled at Joselyn's stammering. She looked so cute, and he couldn't help himself from teasing her. "I'm her boy toy," he whispered with a wink and laughed softly as Joselyn's blush deepened to a dark red. "You know she's got all kinds of money." He shrugged. "She supports me in a life in which I have become accustomed."

Clarisse looked from one to the other; her jaw dropped open and eyes round.

"You're not!" Joselyn squeaked and smacked his arm. "Cheebus, River, don't say things like that. People will believe it." Turning her attention back to the woman, she winced. "He's not my boy toy. He's my, my friend." She turned her gaze to him and smiled. "He's my good friend."

Friend.

River tasted the word and found it wasn't quite right. Okay, yes, he was her friend, but there was more to it besides the whole bodyguard thing. The revelation he had this morning said it all. She was more than a client, more than an acquaintance. She was slowly becoming everything, and it brought forth an unfamiliar feeling. In the twenty years he had served his country, he had known fear on several different levels. Only a fool would not feel anxiety after some of the situations he had found himself. Tracking down terrorists, defusing hostile situations and generally taking care of whatever business his country demanded had given him a healthy respect for fear. But what he was feeling toward the petite author scared him more than all the Taliban in the world. She had wiggled past the walls he had erected until she was bigger than anything else in his universe. If anything happened to her... He slammed a door on the thought. No. Nothing would happen because he wouldn't allow it. He would keep her safe, regardless of the consequences.

He stood to Joselyn's left with his back to the wall, and the remainder of the store spread out before him. Paying little attention to the conversation about storage size and case colors, he scanned the room methodically. People mulled around the brightly lit space, checking out the latest devices. Everything looked normal, so why were the fine hairs on the back of his neck standing at attention? Reaching back, he smoothed them down and resumed his watchful perusal of the area. Several people glanced at him curiously and at the weapon on his hip. Thank God, Louisiana was an open carry state, so nobody questioned its presence. Not that he wasn't as deadly with his bare hands, but the sidearm was a clear warning: It's here for a reason - back off!

"Alright, Ms. Kendrik, I've deactivated your old one and got this one turned on. Restoring everything from the cloud is going to take a few minutes. If you stay here as it finishes, we'll check everything out. In the meantime, I'm going to help another customer. We are so busy today. Saturday afternoons are like this."

Joselyn waved her off, her eyes on the screen as the progress bar inched across. "Please, go ahead. We're fine."

Flashing a grateful smile, Clarisse nodded. "I'll be right back to see you in a few minutes. Just let the update run." Turning, she checked her tablet and moved to an older woman examining earphones.

River chuckled as he heard her ask Clarisse about a pair for her grandson's birthday.

"Have you been to New Orleans before?"

Joselyn's question took him by surprise. When he looked at her, he saw her attention was fixed on the three case boxes in her hand. "It's one of my favorite places," River said. "I have a lot of memories here. See, I have four older sisters but am the only boy. They gave me absolute hell all the time. My mom has pictures of them dressing me up as their own personal little doll. When I got older, my parents, God bless them, had mercy on me and sent me to my Aunt and Uncle's every summer. Their son, Shaun, saved my sanity. We were tight even though he was a couple of years older. So every year from the time I was about ten until I joined the Navy at eighteen, I would spend the summer with him at their farm outside of Meridian. It was long, hard, hot work but man, I loved it. We woke before dawn and worked until the sun went down and it was too dark to see. When he turned sixteen, we started taking trips in his old pickup on the weekends. Usually, we would horse around town or go to the local lake. That year, right before school started, we took off on one last trip and found ourselves in New Orleans. Now, don't get me wrong, I'd been there a few times with my family and the occasional field trip, but two teenagers roaming around was the ultimate adventure. By the time we dragged our butts into the house on Sunday morning, his parents were furious. When I got home later the same night, mine grounded me for a month and threatened never to let me go back. Thank God, they eventually relented. Even with all the trouble we got into, it was worth it. Afterward, it became a tradition of sorts, and we ended our summers here. Mom and Dad pretended to not know about it, and Uncle Aaron made us call him every four hours on the dot to ensure we were alright. It was even the last thing we did together before I left for training."

She leaned against him, placing her hand on his chest. "And what about now?"

He curled his arm around her shoulders, marveling at how well she fit there. "After a long engagement, Shaun got married to the sweetest little angel. They met right out of college and hit it off immediately. I was supposed to be his best man, but we got called away at the last minute. He knew how much it meant to me to serve, so he wasn't angry. They waited until I got back to have a party though. Hannah is a travel nurse so they have this big RV and they travel together. He is a graphic design artist so he can work from anywhere. He called me a couple of months ago and told me they are expecting their first baby. I'm to be the godfather." He puffed his chest out proudly. "Hannah is finishing a contract now, and next month they will head back to Mississippi. He said they are done traveling for a while and are ready to settle down. I envy them because they know what they want. I'm almost forty and have no clue where to go from here."

She leaned against him. "Maybe you should stay here where there are so many good memories," she whispered.

He thought about it a minute and found it didn't freak him out. In fact, settling after two decades of wandering held a certain appeal. He placed a kiss on her head and froze. What did he just do? Taking his gesture in stride, she snuggled closer to his side. He'd figure out everything between them later. He wanted her, and for some reason, she seemed to want him too; everything else was negotiable. "Maybe," he answered.

On the table before them, a ding sounded, and she retrieved her new cell. "All done?" Clarisse had returned and glanced at the screen.

"Looks like it," Joselyn replied.

"Take a minute and check your personal stuff. See if it all downloaded correctly."

Joselyn cradled the cell in her fingers, swiping through contacts and notes. "So far so good. Everything looks to be here." She continued through her calendar before inspecting her photographs. He watched the smile blossom as she glanced through them and her eyes misted over. Looking at her new phone, he saw an older man in many of them and knew they must be the ones of her father. Giving her a bit of privacy, he backed up a step and turned slightly. He was happy she hadn't lost them and would speak to her later about ensuring they wouldn't be in danger again.

"River," she breathed and thrust the phone toward him.

He took the device and looked at the screen. A frown creased his brow as he tried to decipher what he was seeing. There was a picture of a couple standing in a parking lot in front of a large black truck. The photo was grainy, probably due to the low amount of light. Understanding dawned on him as he realized the man standing behind the woman held a gun.

It was a photo of them taken last night in the parking lot.

Quickly he swiped the screen. There was Joselyn, sitting in the hostess stand of the restaurant. Light reflected off the large window as the manager handed her a glass of water.

Next was his truck again, swarming with police as he and Bull stood to the side deep in conversation.

The following picture was of Joselyn sitting at a table, her blonde hair falling over her shoulders as she smiled at a young boy with a copy of her book in his hands. River stood behind her with arms crossed, glaring around the room.

Swipe, she was standing behind him as he shoved Sasha against the wall.

Swipe, Joselyn standing next to a thoroughly enchanted Sasha as they took a selfie.

Each photograph had been taken since she lost her old cell phone. Fury raged in him as he took each one in. But it was the last one which forced a curse from his lips.

It was a close up of them in front of a display of telephone cases. He was looking down at her with a gaze of adoration, his thumb touching her lip. Her eyes were shining brightly as she smiled at him. If he could ignore the whole disturbing ramifications of the picture, it could easily become his favorite photo ever.

Her stalker had her old phone; there was no other excuse. He had used it to take photographs of them, taunting them with his ability to get close to her and posted them to her cloud so she would see them.

His blood turned to ice in his veins, and his training took over. Thrusting the device into her shaking hands, he pushed her gently back into the corner of the store and drew his gun. "Call 911," he hissed as he took a position between her and the rest of the room. Beside them, Clarisse gasped and dropped her tablet. It bounced and shattered before skittering across the floor. A woman noticed the drawn weapon and screamed. Pandemonium erupted. Quickly, the store emptied. Behind him, he heard Joselyn speaking low, the hand against his back trembling. He wanted to pull her into his arms and shelter her from the world but he couldn't. Right now, her safety trumped any personal feelings he had. Nothing else mattered but her.

Chapter 10

It had taken a while, but everything was finally quiet at 2004 Sunset Place. Sitting on the wall overlooking the park, he turned until his back rested against a pillar. Bending his left leg until his foot was flat on the hard surface, he rested his elbow on his knee and turned his gaze toward the east. One road and two large houses separated him from his prey, and one of those was unoccupied. He knew it was because the guest bedroom on the second story currently held his meager belongings.

Closing his eyes, he leaned his head back and grinned. The chaos today at the store was perfect. When the stupid soldier realized how close he had come to losing his charge, he pulled his gun and scared the crap out of everyone there. Afterward, it was easy to walk out of the door with the panicking crowd.

He chortled to himself and slipped off the wall on the housing side, working his way through the silent streets until he stood under the same tree once again. Staring at the two-story house a few doors away, he watched the lights go out one by one until there was only one remaining - Joselyn's room on the top left side.

A thrill raced through him as he thought of the soft comforter of beige and mint green adorning her queen size bed. He had run his fingers over her pillow and even lifted it to smell the unique fragrance that was all her before carefully replacing it exactly as he had found it. Stepping into her closet, he fingered the rows of blouses and pants before turning his attention to one item deep in the back. He hadn't been able to help it. He pulled out the beautiful deep purple dress and hugged it to him. He had meant to leave it behind, once again lost on the rack with the others but he couldn't. It belonged to her, but it also belonged to him.

Remembering it now, he entered the house and made his way to the bedroom in the dark. The owners were on vacation for another few weeks, but he was there legitimately. The elderly couple was paying him to house sit while they were away. It was easy to charm them into believing he was a professional service. Nobody knew his real reason for being there but they would soon.

Closing the blinds tightly and pulling the blackout curtains closed, he turned on a single lamp and sat on the floor. Grabbing a stack of eight by ten papers, he carefully spread them out on the carpeted floor in front of him. Reaching into an envelope, he pulled out the newest offering to his shrine, the same pictures he had taken with her cell phone. He chuckled to himself again before placing the now dead device on top of the photographs. Again, much too easy to obtain what he wanted. Last night, he waited until the soldier had gone to the restroom and paid a busboy ten dollars to drop a plate. While all attention was on the noise, he slipped her cell off the table where she had placed it and into his pocket. She hadn't even noticed it was gone.

Over the next twenty or so minutes, he lost himself in arranging and rearranging the pages until it was perfect. Leaning back, he let his eyes flicker over the three or so dozen photographs telling the story of his love, his obsession. He licked his dry lips and ran a finger over her face. So beautiful. He couldn't wait until she wore his marks and he painted her body with lines and slashes that wept crimson. He couldn't wait to see the tears coursing down her cheeks or the way her eyes would widen in knowing it was her final moments. The taste of her sweat would be intoxicating when it mingled with her fear. He closed his eyes and groaned. Pulling the purple dress to his face, he inhaled but then frowned. It smelled of dust and the cedar of her closet; there was nothing left of her there. This annoyance would soon be taken care of. He would take her lotion, wash, and shampoo the next time he visited her house. He could saturate the fine cloth with her fragrance until he impregnated it with her blood. He had been so excited tonight. Not only did he manage to find the dress, but he had also invaded her personal space for the first time. Laying upon the collage of photographs, he cuddled the dress and closed his eyes. "Joselyn, my sweet little Rose," he whispered reverently into the still room as he reached down his own body. Within moments, he had lost himself in the fantasies of the near future when his fingers would touch her, tease her, torture her.

Reduce her to her essence.

He moaned.

―

Joselyn was exhausted.

Today had gone far beyond normal. Meet and greets always took a lot out of her. In addition to her typical physical weariness, the emotional roller coaster she had just endured added to the overall stress until even her toenails ached.

Curled under her favorite comforter, she hugged her pillow close and stared at the wall. Even as tired as she was, she wasn't sure she would sleep tonight, or ever for that matter. Pulling her knees to her stomach, she clutched the pillow tighter and buried her face into it. Here, in the solitude of her room, she could let go. One thing she had learned over the course of her life was tears could be cathartic. Therefore, she let them flow over her cheeks and disappear into the soft beige of her pillow.

The bed dipped, and she screamed, pulling the pillow away and pushing against an immovable wall beside her. Panting, she balled her fist and pounded against the threat with all her might. Her wrists were caught, and a soothing voice broke through the haze of terror.

"*Shh*, it's me, Joselyn, it's River. I heard you crying and wanted to check on you. It'll be okay."

She stilled, and he let her hands go. Gulping a breath, she lunged at him, wrapping her arms around his waist tightly. He gently stroked her hair as the sobs broke loose in full force. While he held her, she cried for the life she had lost for so long, for her father, and not getting the closure she so desperately needed. Thoughts of her mother and how badly she missed her added to her despair. Her turbulent career with all of its uncertainty haunted her as well. Every fear, concern, doubt, and anguished thought poured from her soul and onto River's shirt-covered stomach.

They stayed that way for a while until the racking sobs turned to hiccupping whimpers and finally silenced. She drew back and laid on the bed staring at the ceiling. She felt the bed shift, and tissues from the box on her bedside table were pressed into her hand. With a grateful half-smile, she wiped her face. She knew she made one ugly crier.

"No, you don't."

She peeked over her hands. "Huh?"

He chuckled. "You said you make for an ugly crier. I don't think so. I think you're breathtakingly beautiful, wet eyelashes, red nose, pink cheeks and all." He smiled and cupped her cheek with his hand. "Stunning, even."

The red currently infusing her cheeks turned a deeper crimson. "I didn't know I said it out loud," she whispered. "I'm so embarrassed."

He smiled at her. "Don't be. You've been through a lot lately. You were due to have a little breakdown. I'd be more shocked if you didn't." He wiped her tear-soaked cheek with one thumb. "I know of hardened soldiers breaking down for a lot less than you've been through. You're so strong and brave. I'm in complete awe of you."

They gazed at each other for a moment. He lowered his head toward her, and her heart stuttered in her chest. This was it, the moment she had thought about and dreamed of for days. This was the moment when she would finally know what it felt like to kiss him. She sighed as he slipped his hand behind her neck and gently nudged her upwards until only a breath separated them.

Joselyn wasn't a complete prude. She had dated a few times, had a couple of boyfriends and one relationship which seemed to be heading toward something much more permanent. Those moments were all "before." Since that summer day when WitSec had appeared at her door and turned her life topsy-turvy, she had been living in a state of waiting. Waiting for her life to regain some control, waiting for her career to be where she wanted, even waiting for someone special to come along and sweep her off her feet. Now she waited on River to move the last quarter inch and take her lips with his.

He searched her face for a moment then let out a groan. She only had a second to wonder what he had seen before his lips pressed against hers. It was tender, sweet, and exactly what she needed, all gentle pressure and soft pulls. Reluctantly he drew back and looked into her eyes again. Apparently, he liked what he saw, for one side of those sinfully sexy lips lifted in a smirk and he quickly dived in again.

Oh, sweet heavens!

The second kiss was not tender, slow and sweet. It was all power, demanding and possessive. As he devoured her mouth, she moaned, parting her lips and he took the opportunity to dive inside, claiming that as well. His kiss was fire, incinerating her until she smoldered and ached.

He pressed her tighter against him, holding her close as if never wanting to let go. In his strong arms, all the fear and doubt evaporated until only overwhelming feelings of rightness remained. She snaked her arms around his neck, slipping her fingers into his hair, gripping tightly with one hand as the other curled around his broad shoulders. His left arm moved around her waist and pulled her into his lap once again. The moment continued, the two of them lost in each other until they couldn't think straight. Eventually, the kiss broke leaving them both panting. Closing her eyes, she threw her head back and was rewarded with kisses and nibbles down the column of her neck to her shoulder.

"Joselyn," he breathed against the tender flesh there.

"Maddox," she breathed his name. She clutched him tightly against her as his hand slid under her shirt and pressed against the skin of her back. His touch seared her to the bone, and she wanted more, needed more. Raking her nails on his shoulder, she dragged them over the broad expanse of his back to the hem before slinking underneath. He groaned again, eyes tightly closed.

Loving the reaction from him, she made herself a promise. From this moment on, she wouldn't call him 'River' again.

"I want you," he whispered against her chin and bit playfully. "I tried to stay away, tried to be strong. You have called me a Frost Giant, but around you, I'm not. When it comes to you, the ice shatters."

Her hands ghosted over his broad back, feeling the rough lines and planes intersected with what must be scars. What had he been through to have so many marks on his skin?

She was pulled back to the moment when his hand started to push her sleeping shirt up. Instantly, she stilled, putting a hand on his to stop him. When he looked at her quizzically, she gulped. "I.. I can't. I'm sorry, I just... I can't."

He froze, hesitated and carefully tugged the shirt over her belly before replacing her back on the bed and putting some distance between them. He took a heaving breath and scrubbed the scruff on his chin. "I'm... Jeez, Joselyn, I didn't mean to get carried away.

I didn't mean to push myself on you. I'm so sorry. It won't happen again, I swear. I thought... No, it doesn't matter what I thought. It was just you and me and... You seemed to want it as much as me. Damn, I'm sorry."

She shook her head with a little laugh and reached out, grabbing his hand. "No, oh gracious, no, goodness, no. You don't understand. It's not that I don't want you because I do. God, I do, so badly. It's not an issue of wanting but more that I haven't, well, you know." Her face flamed bright crimson.

"Oh." A light went on in his eyes as realization dawned. "Ohhh. You're a virgin. Cripes, of course, you are. Don't get me wrong but I wasn't expecting that. You're hot and sexy and in today's age..." He stopped as he recognized the hurt on her face. "No, there's nothing wrong with it, but it's a little bit of a surprise. If you don't mind me being nosey, how have you waited this long?"

She swallowed. "It's all because of my Dad. He was a wonderful man, and I was definitely a 'Daddy's Girl.' He always had time for me. I love both my parents, but he was special, and he never failed to make me feel special." She turned her gaze to her hand. "When I turned twelve, we got dressed in our best clothes, and he took me to dinner. It was a fancy place with a lot of different courses and all these selections of silverware, plates and such. After dinner, he gave me a ring." She held up her left hand and wiggled her fingers showing him a tiny delicate silver band with two hearts set with jewels. "He told me it represented us."

River carefully took her hand and looked at the setting. "It's beautiful."

Joselyn smiled wistfully as she stared at the ring before continuing. "The heart with the sapphire is for him. It's large and protective of the smaller diamond sitting below and to the side. He told me that on one special day, he would watch proudly as this ring is replaced by another. He asked me to let him take care of my heart until the day my husband stepped in. It was so beautiful and special. I wear this ring every day to remind me to remain pure because the one I give my heart to deserves to know he is special to me. I want the person I marry to be my first and my last, my only. My father died before he could see my husband take this off my hand and replace it with his own. I've been tempted many times, but when I see this ring, I remember a special night when a twelve-year-old Joselyn made a promise to her father."

He smiled and squeezed her hand tight. "I understand. I won't lie and say I haven't had my indiscretions, but it doesn't mean I'll judge you in any way. This is special. You deserve to have your dreams come true." Raising her hand to his lips, he pressed them to the palm and nuzzled it with his cheek. "So smart, talented, beautiful and driven. Knowing you want something special with your future doesn't drive me off. It makes you more alluring. The man to win your heart will be the luckiest man on this earth, and I admit it. I envy him, whoever he may be."

Letting her hand go, he gently pressed her back against the pillow and pushed a lock of hair from her face. "Get some sleep. I'm going to check the house and grounds again and call it a night. It's been one hell of a day."

She nodded and watched him ease out of her bedroom and down the hall. Drawing the cover to her chin, she turned on her side and stared at the door. Maddox had called the man she gave her heart to "the luckiest man on earth." He didn't realize that statement had been self-fulfilling. She had already given her heart away and the man retaining it was currently moving around the house below her.

She couldn't pinpoint the moment she had lost it to him, but it didn't matter. She was his and nothing anyone could ever say could change the fact. Maybe it had started the first day in the diner when he stood there all silent and rugged. Perhaps it had been the dozen or so times since when she got a glimpse of the man he was inside. No, it didn't matter when it had, but one thing was certain. It had solidified tonight when he held her as she cried. Understanding why waiting meant so much to her only made her even more sure of her feelings toward Maddox. She looked at the purity ring encircling her finger. In one single action, he had cemented her to him in an unbreakable manner.

She was his.

Chapter 11

*M*addox placed a cup of Joselyn's favorite hot tea on the warming pad by her computer and pressed a kiss to her temple. Snatching a green apple hard candy out of the bowl on her desk, he unwrapped it and popped it in his mouth. "I love these things. You've got me addicted to them."

She grinned and plucked one out of the bowl. Shaking it at him, she shrugged. "These are my 'think rocks.' They help me focus. You keep eating them, and someone is going to have to make a run down to the corner store for more. I'm only a quarter of the way through, and there are only a couple of dozen of these babies left."

He drew his brows together as if contemplating her words. With a shrug, he reached over and grabbed another. "If I must, I must. Whatever keeps you happy." Unwrapping it, he asked, "How's the editing going?"

"Surprisingly good. I think Tia has mellowed out. I can actually find whole passages she didn't mark up. Either I'm getting better, she's calming down, or we are finally clicking. You should have seen my first book she edited. It looked like a crayon factory threw up on it."

He chuckled and dropped into the chair next to her desk, stretching his long legs out before him.

"I like how much calmer you look now. For a while there I was afraid the vein in your temple was going to burst. I swear it was doing the tango."

He settled his hands over his stomach as he happily sucked on the candy. "The house and grounds are secure. You're sequestered in your office where nobody can get to you. Fangasm in Atlanta isn't for another week, and we have a bowl of Happy Orchard's candy to get us through today's editing. Life is good." He winked at her before glancing over at the three screens on the second desk behind her. "And there's Bull at the guard house. I'll go let him in." He eased out of the chair and placed another kiss on her cheek.

She tensed. "Detective Jameson is here?"

"He called a while ago and asked to come by. He has some updates on your case and thought it was safer for him to come here rather than for you to go see him."

She nodded and turned back to her computer. With a few clicks, she saved her work and slid her feet back into her flip-flops. Padding down the hall, she waved at the detective as Maddox opened the door for him. "Detective, hello. Come in, please." She motioned toward the living room. "Have a seat. Can I get you anything? Coffee? Tea?" She smirked at Maddox, "Happy Orchard green apple candy?"

The last comment earned her a playful growl from her normally brooding bodyguard.

Detective Jameson either didn't hear her candy comment or ignored it. Instead, he declined the refreshments and motioned for her to sit. He looked frazzled. Joselyn frowned as her stomach churned. Whatever he had to say, she was pretty sure she wasn't going to like it.

He placed a folder on the coffee table before him and drummed his fingers on it. Blowing out a breath, he nodded to himself, leaned forward and braced his forearms on his knees. Without any preamble, he started.

"First off, I contacted a friend who knows computers inside and out. I asked him to check into her old cell. The phone wasn't used while it was missing. According to him, the only time the cloud was accessed was at the restaurant and the cell phone store. He put a watch on it for me, but we both doubt that it will be turned back on so it can't be traced. Basically, it's a dead end."

"Damn," Maddox swore then apologized. "Sorry, Joselyn. What else do you have, Bull?"

"I've been working on her case for a while, and I think I may have an idea who the stalker is. Now, it's not set in stone, but due to certain circumstances, I have an idea. A damn good idea at that."

"Circumstances? What circumstances?" Joselyn frowned.

"Okay. Here goes." He mumbled under his breath. "Ms. Kendrik... Joselyn... I got to thinking about what you said. All through this, you have been very insistent this stalker had to be Douglas McClane. The only problem with your theory is Douglas McClane has been dead for more than a year now. There are reports of the shootout in the cemetery and crime scene photographs. We even obtained an identification by his last surviving relative, a cousin named Donavan Beecher. This brings me back to my theory. I'm pretty sure it's Beecher who is following you. I think he's trying to finish what McClane started."

Joselyn felt her stomach clench. Douglas McClane had a cousin. "A cousin?" she asked incredulously.

Detective Jameson opened the folder and pulled out several photographs. He turned one around and pushed it toward Joselyn and Maddox sitting side by side on the sofa. "This is Douglas McClane."

The photo was one she had seen many times before. It was the one most news outlets used during the trial. In the professional shot taken about eight years ago, McClane sat stiffly against a muted backdrop of mottled gray and dark blue. Wearing a buttoned dress shirt complete with tie and tie bar, he glared solemnly into the camera lens with a cold, calculating stare. As always, a chill raced up her spine. She knew he had been a high school literature teacher for years before his capture and conviction; that thought still scared the crap out of her. This cold-blooded, calculating, serial rapist and murderer had held influence over hundreds of impressionable young minds. It sickened her, and she rubbed her arms to ward off the chills again racing along them before turning her gaze away.

"This one is Donavan McClane Beecher." Detective Jameson dropped another photograph next to the other.

Joselyn leaned forward and studied the picture intently. It was a snapshot like one would use for a passport or work identification badge. In it, Beecher wore a polo type shirt with the top two buttons undone and the barest hint of a white tee-shirt peeking out. There were a lot of amazing familial similarities between the two. Even if Detective Jameson hadn't told her they were related, it would have been obvious in the photographs. The slope of the forehead was the same as were the too thin lips and pointed chins. McClane's hair was a medium brown and straight. Beecher's dirty blonde sported gentle waves throughout. Beecher's nose was a little wider and his cheekbones a tiny bit lower. The most striking difference was the eyes. McClane's dark hazel looked coldly sinister. Beecher's were a few shades lighter and conveyed a more caring warmth. She sat back in her seat.

Beside her, Maddox picked up both photographs and studied them carefully. "This makes a lot of sense. How sure are you?"

Taking the photographs from Maddox's hands, Jameson placed them back into the folder as he continued. "Almost positive. There are too many coincidences for it not to be a viable possibility. I'm sure you noticed how closely they resembled each other. Their mothers were fraternal twins, and when they married, each had only one child. The women named their sons with the middle name of the other's surname. The two boys were extremely close, born three months apart and raised next door to each other almost as brothers. According to neighbors who knew both men as they grew up, one was never seen without the other. They remained close until McClane went off to college and obtained double masters in literature and teaching while Beecher went to trade school to become a journeyman electrician."

River jumped in with the question bouncing around in Joselyn's mind. "Why do you think Beecher is her stalker?"

"The two were close growing up. They even shared a couple of girlfriends in school. Beecher identified his cousin's body. As soon as it was released, he had his cousin cremated. He has since vanished. I spoke to his employer. He hasn't been seen in months. His apartment manager said he was never late on rent but after his cousin died, he only came by one time to pick up some personal items. He broke the lease and told the manager to do whatever he wanted with the furnishings. Then there's this." He pulled out another set of six photographs and splayed them out over the table. In them were six identical necklaces consisting of a small round puffed disk with a dove engraved on the front of a delicate silver chain. Hesitating a moment, he pulled out a seventh photo, but this one depicted a piece of paper with writing on it. Joselyn read the words, and her blood ran cold.

Six Blossoms, six Doves
Six times to fall in love
Gossamer wings learned to fly
Seven's time now draws nigh.

The writing was the same, the exact same. This note was penned by the man who had been stalking her. "Donavan Beecher," she said in a shaky voice.

The detective nodded. "Or, at least we are pretty

sure it was him. These are memorial necklaces. Inside each disk are a few grams of ashes. They are human, though who they belong to, we can't say. I have a gut feeling it's Douglas McClane."

River's face took on his hard, Frost Giant persona. "Who received the necklaces?"

"They arrived yesterday, special delivery to the mothers of Douglas McClane's victims." He flinched a moment as if trying to figure out the best way to continue. With a sigh, he spilled the words out in a rush. "These were special order items, hand-made by a silversmith in Nevada and extremely easy to track. We contacted him to get some information. He told us they were ordered three months ago by a man in Florida who identified himself as John Michaels."

"Deidre's love interest in my books." Joselyn felt the room tilt. Steeling her nerves, she swallowed. "Okay, keep going."

"These things are not cheap. We're talking he paid three hundred dollars each for them."

"Eighteen hundred dollars to send a message?" Maddox wrinkled his brow. "It doesn't make sense."

Jameson winced. "No, not eighteen hundred, twenty-one hundred. He ordered seven of them."

The stillness of the room was shattered when Maddox leaped to his feet and swore. He paced back and forth, scrubbing his face with his hand and pushing his fingers through his hair. He continued striding around the room until he finally stopped in front of Joselyn. Dropping to one knee, he took her cold hands in his and squeezed gently.

"You know I'll protect you, don't you? You know no matter what, nothing is ever going to happen to you." He searched her eyes. "Please tell me you know this."

She swallowed and looked at their clasped hands. Here, in her house, was the only place she felt safe and a big part of it was because of this man kneeling in front of her. Slowly she raised her head and nodded. "I know," she whispered. "I know you will do everything in your power to keep me safe. I know nothing will touch me or hurt me as long as you're here. It doesn't mean the thought of Donavan Beecher already purchasing a necklace with his psychopath cousin's ashes for my mother doesn't scare the living daylights out of me though."

He lifted her hands to his lips and kissed them. Letting one go, he grasped the other and turned toward his friend and former team member. "Now what?"

"Considering everything we've learned, I felt it prudent to get everyone up to speed. I've contacted her former handler with WitSec, Jonathan Hanger. After briefing him on what we know and suspect he wasn't too happy. He said given the nature of the threat, he can easily get her back into the program until Beecher is caught."

Joselyn shook her head. "No."

"Joselyn," Maddox said softly. "Maybe it's a good idea."

"No!" She pulled her hand out of his and stood. Pacing back and forth, she chewed on her thumb.

"I'm not going back into witness protection. I'm not! Douglas McClane stole three years of my life. Three I'll never get back. Now I'm finally starting to find my place again, and his cousin wants to send me back under a rock? Not happening. As I said, I trust Maddox completely. He has made this place into a fortress nobody can breach. I'll take extra precautions not to allow myself to be put into a position where Beecher can get to me. I have to go to the convention in Atlanta this weekend, but I'll cancel the one next month as well as the three upcoming public appearances. I think I have two podcast interviews in the coming week, but they can be done remotely from here." She nodded and continued to pace. "Yeah, that will work. I'll go crazy from cabin fever, but it's better than the alternative."

Maddox stopped her and pulled her into his arms. She melted against him and laid her head against his shoulder. "I'm so proud of you, honey. So damn proud! I know this isn't easy for you, but I promise I'm not going to leave your side. Look at this situation like a golden opportunity for you to get in some serious writing. And, when the cabin fever gets to be too much, I'll figure out a way to safely get you the space you need. In the meantime, I'll ply you with hot tea and green apple candy to your heart's content."

His comment did what he intended, and she relaxed marginally. Chuckling softly, she stepped out of his arms. "Just not at the same time because that would be kind of gross."

He laughed, the deep rumble which always made her toes curl and her heart skip. Maddox didn't laugh nearly enough, but she had hopes once Donavan

Beecher was caught, she would see what she could do to put a few more laughs into his life. He deserved it, and so did she.

A cough drew their attention, and she started. For a moment, she had forgotten Detective Jameson was still there.

"Well, if you do leave the house, let me know, and I'll get a couple of beat cops to help keep an eye on things. As it is, we've scheduled more drive-bys with marked cars in your neighborhood. I talked to your HOA, and they are going to increase security measures for the time being by hiring an extra guard for the gates. I've given them a picture of Beecher so they can be on the lookout for him."

"Great, my dues are going to double," she quipped.

"Double or not, it's better to be safe than sorry. You're in a good community here with a lot of safety measures already built in. A few more won't hurt, and it will keep your neighbors vigilant." Detective Jameson stood and gathered his file together. They followed him to the door and stopped when he did. "When I asked River to come help out here, I seriously thought it would be just a few days of him making a presence around you until this yokel got tired and moved on. Now I know it isn't some random guy, I'm happier he's here. Joselyn, you couldn't have anyone better watching your six than Maddox Benson."

They said their goodbyes as Detective Jameson opened the door and exited. She punched in her code to rearm the system and turned to Maddox. "Alright, we have a name. Now what?"

"Now, we hunker down, stay vigilant and wait."

Chapter 12

Watching Joselyn work was quickly becoming one of River's favorite things to do. She was well organized, calm and knew exactly what she was doing, even in the frantic bustle of forty authors setting up booths for the Atlanta Fangasm. Placing the last box of books on the floor under the table, he stepped back and took in the tangible excitement of a successful author's world.

She stacked the books carefully on the table, removed several mugs, pens, bookmarks and assorted other swag from their boxes and placed them to the side. Arranging them carefully, she looked over her table, stepped in and arranged them again. After the fourth time, she muttered something under her breath which sounded like, "off balance" before starting again.

River was hyper-aware of every person who took a step toward their little area in the corner. When they had first arrived, he took one look at her booth location and had balked. It was bad enough she insisted on coming after everything she had been through, but the original booth locale was not going to cut muster. She had been placed front and center of the massive room with access on all sides. What followed had been extremely stressful. She stomped her foot and glared at him as he insisted on loading her back into his truck and turning right around for

New Orleans if she couldn't see reason. The heated discussion drew several looks until they moved into a back hallway out of view. He explained to her there was absolutely no way he would ever be able to relax with the present setup. Finally understanding his position, she relented and called the event organizers. Once she explained the situation to them, they were happy to exchange her location with another author - one who was overjoyed to be placed in the more desirous location. Joselyn wasn't as happy in the back corner since she had specifically requested the more visible location at registration. "If it keeps that glowering look off your face, it's worth it," she had told him. "Women want their hunky models to be sexy, not snarling. Well, unless he's a shifter but I don't write in that genre."

Her attempt at humor had fallen flat. River simply was not happy and wished he could take her back home where he could control the situation better. He knew there would be precious little sleep for him over the next few days.

A cold bottle of water was thrust into his hand. "Relax. I think you're more uptight about this thing than I am. You just have to stand there and look all smoldering hot. I have to talk to these people and play nice."

"Alright. I'll try to behave," he agreed. "Is it okay if I only growl at the men?"

She tapped her lip with one finger. "Only if they get fresh. Otherwise, they will think I'm taken."

He arched an eyebrow at her as if to say, "Aren't you?"

She swallowed at the heated stare and fiddled with the array of permanent pens on the table. Glancing at her watch, she took a deep breath. "Almost time," she muttered as she sat.

Kneeling beside her, he opened a small box and pulled out a little crystal bowl. He placed it beside her hand. "There, now it's perfect."

She opened the top and the smile she flashed him could rival the sun. "Oh, Maddox, how thoughtful!" Inside were her favorite green apple candies in their little individual wrappers.

"There's a whole bag under here. I thought it would be a nice way to share a little bit of yourself with your readers." He placed a kiss on her cheek. Plucking one out, he unwrapped it. "And it has nothing at all to do with my own addiction." He popped it into his mouth with a wink. "Good luck," he told her as he stood again, taking a step back against the wall beside her banner. Crossing his arms over his chest, he adopted the persona Joselyn had nicknamed, "Frost Giant." She could call it whatever she liked, as long as nobody got too close.

Over the course of the next four hours, Joselyn signed autographs, distributed books, took photos and spent time with her fans. It was nerve-wracking for him, and he tensed every time a man moved toward her, but he knew he couldn't suffocate her. So he manned up, kept a close vigilance and remained silent.

"Jos, Jos, Jos!"

A vivacious woman of approximately five-foot-three with bright red curls piled on top of her head, and sparkling green eyes behind a pair of black horn-rimmed glasses jogged over and dropped her bag beside the table. As Joselyn stood, the new woman threw her arms around her and hugged hard. Plopping into the empty chair, she let out a huff and fanned herself with a paperback copy of *Mayhem and Mixed Nuts, Deidre Files Book Two* from the table.

"What are you doing shoved back in this corner? I know you had booth nine reserved yet here you are clear down in the nether regions of the thirties. What gives?"

Joselyn rolled her eyes and nodded toward River. "Security."

The woman's jaw dropped. "Oh my stars, is this the infamous River I've heard so much about? Well of course it is." She stood and shoved her hand at him. "Annabeth Switcher. I'm Jos's agent."

River took her hand and shook it. "Nice to meet you Annabeth. I have heard quite a bit about you as well."

"Lies, every bit of it," Annabeth joked as she retrieved the book to fan herself again. "Gracious, it's hotter than a turkey's butt in November. Doesn't the air work in here?" She eyed River and pursed her lips. "You're one seriously good-looking man. I don't normally handle models, but I would make an exception for you. I bet we could have you on the cover of a dozen books by Christmas." She dug into her bag and pulled out a card. "Here, you call me, and I'll get it set up."

River looked at the card she had thrust into his hand. "I don't think..."

"It's okay honey; you don't have to think. Just flex those muscles and look smoldering. The photographers will do the rest." She poked at River's bicep and squealed. "Delicious." She hesitated for a moment as a frown creased her brow. "Where was I? Oh yes, Jos, are you planning on going to the party tonight?"

River chuckled to himself. Joselyn's agent was a handful, no doubt. However, she had a certain enduring quality as well. He studied her as she sat talking to Joselyn between fan visits. Shorter than Joselyn but a few more curves, she reminded him of his sister, Marla, and shook his head. Watching the two together, he could see them hitting it off as well.

"Oh, you have to come to the party. It's only going to be an hour. Margaret, Bethany, and Delilah are all going to be there. I know you don't want to miss it. Remember St. Louis last fall?" She wiggled her eyebrows suggestively.

Joselyn looked at him. "I don't know. Maddox wants to keep my outings as few as possible."

Annabeth winked at him. "You'll bring her, and I'm sure she'll be safe with all those muscles at her side. Knowing the women who will be there tonight, you will be in more danger then she will. It's mostly romance writers. Their minds stay in the gutter, bless their little hearts."

Maybe it was the grin on Annabeth's face reminding him of Marla, or maybe it was the hopeful plea on Joselyn's, but he nodded. "Okay. We can go for a little bit. I'd hate to disrupt your fun. You have to listen to whatever I say, though."

Annabeth stood and pushed against his arm. "Nothing is going to happen. It's a private party with the authors and other literary professionals. Oh which reminds me, I saw Tia in the lobby. She was rushing off for something or another, but I knew you two hadn't met yet. She's going to be there, too. Seeing as you two drive each other up a wall, it's high time you met, don't you think?"

"Tia? That's wonderful. I'd love to meet the woman who reins in my words finally."

"Good, good." She glanced down at her cell. "I need to take care of a few things before the party. See you at six in ballroom two."

She started to walk off, stopped and returned. With a sheepish grin, she dropped the book she had been using as a fan on the table. "I'd forget my head if it weren't glued on tight. See you tonight," she called out and disappeared into the crowd.

"So, that was Annabeth?" River asked with a chuckle.

"Yep, that was Annabeth."

"She's what my father calls, 'tiny but mighty.' Reminds me a bit of my aunt and my sister." He lifted his chin toward the table. "Alright, Ms. Author, you have a line forming. It's only forty-five minutes left, so get busy."

She smiled at him one of those breathtaking smiles of hers. "Aye, aye, Sir," she said as she snapped a salute.

He shook his head and resumed scanning the room. Less than an hour to go and he could finally relax in their suite for a bit before the party. As much as he wished he could shield her, he knew he couldn't deny letting her go when she spent so much time alone. The outing would do her good. However, he would feel a lot better when he could hide her away in her house where nobody could get to her except him.

The thought of touching her made his breath catch. Since the night she rebuked him, he had been careful to avoid a similar circumstance again. It was hard, no pun intended, to keep his hands to himself. Even now, he wanted to reach out and stroke her hair, to nuzzle her neck and hear her make those little sighs of happiness whenever they spent time alone. Forcing his mind back to the crowded room before him, he pushed those thoughts away. Joselyn's safety demanded his attention just as his heart was fast becoming as demanding for the woman, herself. He would be glad when this was all over because he was going to do whatever he could to bind her to him. Earlier today, when she commented about being taken, he wanted to tell her she most definitely was taken but it wasn't the time nor the place to have that discussion. They would soon because he had made up his mind. She'll be his, no doubts about it.

At exactly six o'clock, River stood outside of ballroom two with Joselyn on his arm. After the day's signing session had ended at five, they had packed her table contents into the boxes underneath. River wanted to bring everything to her room but she assured him the doors would be locked and nobody would be allowed inside; everything was safe. However, as they started to leave, he grabbed the bag of candies. The incident with the strawberries reminded him to keep anything she may be consuming close by.

"Okay," she murmured turning to him. "This shouldn't take long. Think of it as a cocktail party. People will be mingling, talking and usually, drinking. Don't be nervous."

He chuckled. "Are you talking to yourself or me? Honey, I've been to many balls and formal gatherings while I was in the service." His eyes wandered over her. "You look stunning, by the way."

And she did. She had put her hair up into a fancy arrangement with little ringlets framing her beautiful face. The makeup she wore was light, a bit of dark gold on her eyes and a little more underneath making the whiskey colored depths pop. It didn't look like she had put anything on her cheeks and her lips were pink and glossy. The dress was what his sisters referred to as 'the little black dress every woman needs.' It hugged her body from the Mandarin collar to just above her knees with three quarter length sleeves and made of some shimmery fabric. He lost his ability to speak when she turned around. It was open with soft folds framing the creamy expanse of her back ending with a gentle swoop of gathered fabric resting above her rear. She'd finished the outfit with a pair of black heels, a tiny wristlet to keep her cell, and some simple stud earrings.

The smile she gave him was dazzling. "Thank you, Maddox. You look pretty awesome yourself and thanks for not refusing to wear a suit." She smoothed the lapels of the dark blue jacket and fidgeted with the two-tone gray tie. "Handsome."

Lifting her hand, he pressed his lips to her fingers. "I love hearing you say my name. Do it again."

Her cheeks flushed, and a seductive little smile graced her lips. She pulled her bottom lip into her teeth and breathed, "Maddox."

He groaned and closed his eyes. "Woman, what you do to me." Pulling her into his arms, he lowered his face and took her lips in his. He kissed her in a gentle, sweet brush and nipped the bottom. Letting her go he pulled back slightly. "Green apple lip gloss?"

She nodded.

He leaned in and licked her lips again before sucking the bottom into his mouth. "MMM. There's no doubt about it; it's my favorite flavor." He whispered huskily. "Come on, let's go before I forget I'm a gentleman and whisk you off somewhere quiet and secluded and do things to make us both blush."

"I sincerely doubt much would make you blush, Maddox," she whispered.

"Minx," he groaned again, closing his eyes and steeling himself. Taking her hand, he tucked it into the crook of his arm and opened the door to the ballroom.

As they walked in, the sudden hush turned into a loud yell of "Surprise!"

He almost lost it when several people jumped toward them. Immediately, he yanked her behind him and reached for his gun only to realize he had left it locked in the safe in their suite. He swore. She had begged him to leave it behind for the party citing it was secluded and safe. He wouldn't be doing it again.

"Relax big guy," Annabeth laughed bouncing over with something pink and tropical in her hand. "It's a little birthday party for Joselyn. Happy birthday, honey."

He blinked. Was it her birthday? Crap! How did he not know it? "It's your birthday?"

She dropped her chin. "Yeah."

"Mother..." he stopped at the glare she gave him. "Trucker," he finished lamely. "I didn't know. I feel like such a jerk."

"How could you know?" The color of her face turned an even darker shade of red. "I haven't exactly advertised it."

"If I had known, I would have gotten you something."

She pressed her hand against his chest. "You did. I have a big bag of green apple candy waiting for me in my room. Honestly, it was so thoughtful of you. Thank you again."

They looked at each other for several heartbeats until Annabeth pushed them gently toward a table in the middle of the room. The cake upon it was a beautiful pink and mint with fuchsia stargazer lilies framing the center. He read the white icing letters therein.

Happy 28th Birthday, Joselyn

Wait. Was she twenty-eight? That meant he was ten, almost eleven years older than her. A muttered curse slipped through his lips, and he took a step back. It never occurred to him she would be so much younger. It wasn't as if she looked older but the way she carried herself, he had assumed she would be about thirty or thirty-two at the most. An eight-year gap he could handle. But no, she was twenty freaking eight years old! That made him a dirty old man, a creeper, a cradle robber. He pushed his fingers through his hair. He was falling in love with a girl who was still in elementary school when he had graduated high school and joined the military. Cripes.

He took in several deep breaths. He needed to think. No, he needed to do his damn job and keep Joselyn, keep his *client*, safe. He can figure out everything else later.

"Maddox?"

He gave Joselyn a nod and clasped his hands behind his back. "Yes?"

Her eyes clouded. "What's wrong? The Frost Giant is back."

"Just doing my job. Enjoy yourself; I'll keep an eye on everything."

Her bottom lip trembled, but she drew herself together. "Alright." She turned away to join her author friends and acquaintances. Looking over her shoulder, he could see the hurt swimming in her gaze. The look, along with the hesitant way she had spoken almost made him go to his knees, but he made himself stand strong. He had to put some space between them before somebody got hurt. He knew age difference didn't matter to other people, but she wasn't 'other people.' She was Joselyn, a woman who had already been through too much in her short, *twenty-eight-year* lifespan. She did not need to be saddled with an old man like him. He couldn't do that to her. He had to take a step back before it was too late.

The problem was, it was already too late.

Chapter 13

*J*oselyn had no idea what she had done wrong, but whatever it was, it must have been bad. Sitting on the passenger side of Maddox's truck, she stared out the window, watching the passing scenery. Ever since the first night at the party, he had become withdrawn, and every attempt by her to engage him in conversation had fallen flat. He remained courteous and even helpful throughout the three-day conference, but something fundamental had changed between them. No longer did he call her Joselyn, choosing "Ma'am" and "Ms. Kendrik" instead. Gone were the smoldering gazes and the "accidental" brush of hands as they worked together to set up her table each day. She missed the easy manner in which they had gotten along. She missed *him*. Along with his tenderness, the small bit of peace she had acquired evaporated. When the nightmares visited before, he would suddenly appear and wake her with a kiss or a caress, ensuring her she was safe, secured, and cared for. Last night she awoke in the middle of the night, sweaty and panting, her pillow still wet as she struggled to disentangle her legs from the sheets. She saw the light go on in the sitting room connecting their bedrooms. A shadow blocked out the light shining under the door but after a moment, it withdrew, and the light turned off. The absence of his comfort hurt most of all.

"River," she tried again. "Maddox?"

He grunted.

She sighed and turned to face him. "Please, will you tell me what I did wrong?"

He never took his eyes off the road. "You didn't do anything wrong, Ms. Kendrik."

That's it. She was tired, her heart hurt, and she felt rejected. Curling her hands into fists, she closed her eyes and screamed inwardly. "Pull over." Her voice was cold and full of fury.

"We are almost to New Orleans."

"Pull. Over. Now."

"I'm sorry, Ms. Kendrik, but that's not an option," River stated flatly. "We are too exposed out here, and your house is less than an hour away. Unless it's an emergency, it can wait until you're safely inside your home."

She glared at him. "Fine but you better be ready, *Mr. Benson*, because you and I are having a long talk. I'm already ticked off so another hour of simmering should put me right about to boiling." She turned and glared out the window, watching the miles race by. She was going to get some answers and soon because this situation wasn't working for her.

Traffic coming off the I-10 was congested because of an accident. Instead of an hour to brood, Joselyn got almost two. Stomping into her house, she threw her bag on the table, kicked off her shoes and disappeared into the kitchen. Breaking out the bottle of red, she poured herself a full glass before gulping half of it.

"Do you think it's a good idea to drink on an empty stomach?"

Her look threw daggers. "Believe me; you want me to be a little mellow." She tipped the glass back, finished it and poured another to the halfway mark.

Maddox turned. "I'll go get your boxes in."

"Leave the damned boxes," she growled. "You and I need to talk."

He sighed and pushed his hands through his hair. "I don't think..."

She snorted. "That's obvious."

Pushing past him, she went into the living room and dropped onto the sofa. She tucked her feet under her and braced the glass on her leg. "Sit."

One of those deliciously dark eyebrows quirked at her order. Normally, she would have giggled or teased, but right now she was plain mad. "Sit. Down," she repeated a little more forcibly and took another drink of her wine. She barely resisted the urge to throw the glass at him when he sat ramrod straight in the chair across from her.

"Alright, something has pissed you off, made you mad, upset you, or something. Until Thursday night, you were sweet, kind, and attentive. Suddenly, you became the Frost Giant again, and frankly, I don't know why. All I do know is this: I have whiplash from your mood swings, and I'm freaking tired of it. You're going to tell me what's going on!"

He studied her a moment before slowly shaking his head. "Nothing is going on, Ms. Kendrik."

Fury burned through her. "The hell there's not. Did you hear me? I've cursed twice in the last two minutes. It's more than I have in the past year. I'm that confused and upset! Something is bothering you, and I want to know what it is." She dropped her face into her hands as the anger drained out of her. "Please? Maddox, please won't you talk to me? Tell me what I did to make you so mad that you can barely stand to look at me. I can't take this. It's killing me."

His mouth opened and closed. He blinked, his face showing more emotion than she had seen all weekend. The protective glare was still there, but it was tempered with a bit of sorrow. He looked as if he had lost something precious. Setting the glass on the table, she slid to her knees, knelt before him and place a hand on his leg. "Maddox?"

His hand covered hers, and for a second, she thought it was going to be alright. Warm and comforting, her breath caught as she looked with longing at his hand resting so protectively over hers. The moment passed, and he pulled his hand away letting the cold demeanor slide over him again.

Her heart broke. Whatever was going on with him, he refused to share it with her. Rising to her feet, she turned away. Stopping in the doorway, she looked back at him. "If you're going to close yourself off from me, I think it's time for you to go," she whispered. "I'd rather go into WitSec again than return to what we were before. I can't live like this. I just... I can't. You mean too much to me now. I could face anything because I knew you would be there for me, taking care of me, standing by me, being my rock when the demons circled. But knowing you can't stand to be in the same room with me," she shook her head sadly. "I've given you too much already, and I can't be here in this house with you and turn off how I feel. It's not possible. So if you insist on keeping yourself withheld from me, you need to leave, and I'll call Jonathan tomorrow. I'll go back into protection until this thing is through."

He shot to his feet, reaching for her but let his hand drop. It became obvious he was contemplating walking out of her life instead of discussing whatever it was bothering him. It hurt. She felt her heart shatter, and her soul ripped in two, but she stood her ground. Even though she wanted to run to him, to pull him into her arms and hold him, she couldn't. Whatever was causing this rift between them was on him, and he had to address it. So she waited, watching the emotions as they washed across his handsome face.

"Eleven years."

In an instant, the decision had been made, and he dropped into the chair. Leaning forward, he braced his elbows on his knees and ran both hands through his hair.

"Excuse me?" Her brow furrowed. "I don't understand."

He looked at her. "Eleven years. I didn't realize you were so much younger than me. Until I saw the cake, it never occurred to me there was such an age difference between us. You carry yourself more mature than twenty-eight. I thought you were at least thirty or thirty-two."

"Okay, there are eleven years between us. I fail to see where it matters."

Maddox stood and started to pace. "Can't you see? It matters. I'm almost forty, Joselyn. I'm retired from the military. While you were going to sleepovers and learning how to drive, I was already several tours into my service!"

"I wasn't a big fan of sleepovers."

He closed his eyes and growled. "That's not the point. The year I graduated high school and enlisted, you were in second grade. *Second grade*, Joselyn. I was an adult, and you were only a child. I'm too old for you, too old to saddle you with a busted ex-sailor covered in scars both inside and out. Look at you. You're a successful author with a bright future. Your whole life is waiting for you."

With a snarl, Joselyn darted over until she stood toe to toe with him and dropped to sit on the coffee table. "Yes, Maddox, my whole life is waiting for me. You're right about that, but it's the only thing you're right about. You forgot something there. It is MY life. Mine. You can't tell me how to live it. My Lord, I'm currently hiding in this house because someone else thinks they have the right to dictate to me, and now you're doing the same? So what if you're eleven years older. So what if you're retired from the military and my career is starting. So what!" She screamed and slapped at the wetness trickling down her cheeks. "You may be older than me, "she continued, "but it doesn't matter because I know the kind of man you are. You're protective, funny, loyal and strong." She poked him in the chest. "In here beats the heart of the man I care about and it doesn't matter to me if that heart is thirty-eight or eighty-eight. Age is just a number."

"A pretty big number," he retorted.

She threw her head back and furiously roared. He made her so mad! Here she was wondering what had upset him and it was her freaking age? Seriously?

"You know what? To be so much older and wiser, you're really slow sometimes."

He rubbed his chest where she had poked it. "What would your mother say if she knew?"

"She wouldn't say anything. Maddox, my father was thirteen years older than my mother. He and her brother, my uncle Max, were best friends their whole lives. So see, it's probably genetic. We Kendrik women like our men aged to perfection."

Seeing the stunned look on his face melted away the anger until she felt only bone-deep exhaustion. Cupping his face, she turned it to her. "I know you're trying to come to terms with this, but seriously, it's not a big deal. If two people care for each other, age doesn't matter. If it doesn't bother me, it shouldn't bother you, and it doesn't matter one bit what other people say." Joselyn stopped and took a cleansing breath before continuing. "You know, my Mom was a pretty smart cookie. She said that God, in his infinite wisdom, sometimes did things we could not understand. She was a firm believer in thinking that He created someone who would be perfect for each of us. Sometimes, it was at the same time, but sometimes one of them had to age a little first. Mom and dad knew each other their whole lives but only fell in love later. They got married when she was twenty-three, and I came along when she was twenty-nine. They had thirty-three wonderful years together before he died and though she misses him terribly, she wouldn't trade one moment for all the gold in the world. That's the kind of love I want. I'd rather have one year with somebody I love than to spend thirty years with someone I just got along with." She mentally slapped herself when she realized what she had said. In an attempt to cover those hasty words, she stood and gave him a warm smile. "I'm tired. I got no sleep last night, and the drive home stressed me out. I'm going to take a long soak in the tub and order from Giovanni's. Afterward, I'm going to take a nice nap, and when I wake up maybe we can continue this conversation, yeah?"

Maddox seemed to finally understand what she was saying because he stood up, cupped his hand around the nape of her neck, massaging it gently. With a sigh, he nodded. "Yeah."

They stared at each other a moment then he pulled her to him and lowered his lips to hers. She had been kissed tenderly. She had been kissed passionately. This time, she got desperation. She could feel the turmoil in him finally release as he claimed her once again. Lips mashed together so hard their teeth almost touched. It was wild, consuming and she freaking loved it.

Panting, he pulled away, and the fire she had gotten so used to seeing in his icy blues was back. Thank God! Her knees threatened to buckle as she clung to him.

"I thought I was doing what was right. I thought I needed to pull back, to give you options. I want you to be happy, even if it wasn't with me. I'm sorry if I hurt you," Maddox said earnestly.

"You thought wrong. I'm not a child, Maddox. I'm an adult who knows what I want. I don't want options. I want you. You did hurt me, but you're forgiven. Please, don't do it again."

He flashed her a half smirking grin making her belly clench. Pressing his forehead against hers, he said, "Yes, Ma'am. Go get your bath; I'll call Giovanni's so it'll be here by the time you get out."

Joselyn's heart stuttered and a weight lifted off her shoulders. "Alright." She pulled back and caressed his cheek. "Thank you for taking care of me."

"Forever."

There was strength in that single word. It was not only an affirmation but a promise. Joselyn knew Maddox was letting her know he would not only take care of her physically but emotionally as well. Turning away, she climbed the stairs to her bedroom and went into her bath. Filling the tub with hot water, she dropped in a lavender and tulip bomb, watching it fizz as it dispersed. Re-entering her bedroom, she went to her bedside table to retrieve her mp3 player and stopped dead in her tracks. Something looked wrong with her bed, so she turned on the lamp. A gasp escaped and all the blood drained from her head, making her stumble slightly. Slowly, her eyes took in what her brain attempted to comprehend. Her beige and mint green comforter had been slashed to shreds along with several of the matching pillows. Scattered over the surface and dipping into the rents and holes were the contents of those pillows along with hundreds of dried rose petals. The one intact pillow hosted something small and shiny. She leaned in to get a better look and drew back in shock. A silver necklace rested on the surface. The finely crafted chain dipped in the creases where she normally laid her head, and the spherical pendant glinted in the meager lamplight. Without a doubt, she knew it would contain human remains. It looked exactly like the ones Detective Jameson had shown them last week except for one thing. Where all the others had a dove carved upon the surface, this one had a beautiful rose in breathtaking detail. Beside it was a piece of paper with a picture of her and Maddox, eyes on each other as they stood outside the door to ballroom two. A big red heart had been drawn around her face, but several long slashes ripped through his. Beneath the picture, words had been angrily stroked.

> *The soldier broods and walks the night,*
> *To save the Rose, his hopeless fight.*
> *He pursues her now, in an attempt to steal,*
> *That which is MINE, to worship, to kill.*
> *Time draws short; Harvest is soon,*
> *For Soldier and Rose to meet their doom.*

There was a scream, and it took a moment for her to register it came from her own throat. In a flash, Maddox was there with his weapon drawn, one arm pulling her close to his side. He saw her bed and let out a curse. In the space of one second, everything slammed into her. Images flittered through her brain - the bloody roses, strawberries, Detective Jameson's skeptical face, River's Frost Giant glare, her bed with the ripped and torn sheets, certain words from each poem blinking brighter and brighter.

Bloody

Fear

Death

Harm

Feast

Doom

Kill

Kill

Kill

Joselyn squeezed her eyes tightly against the mental assault. "No," she moaned as the flickering vision was replaced by one even more sinister- a black tunnel with Douglas McClane's dead eyes morphing into the laughing ones of Donavan Beecher. She trembled and shook until her teeth rattled. Someone was speaking, but she couldn't understand what they were. She gasped, unable to catch a breath. Panic devoured her in its frozen jaws.

Little Rose

Little Rose

Little Rose

Douglas' condescending tone whispered in her ears.

The arms around her tightened and shook her, but she couldn't respond. Maddox. It had to be him as he was always there. He was the one who sheltered her. He was the one who protected her. He was the one who stood between her and the rest of the world. It was only fitting, then, that Maddox caught her as her eyes rolled back, her knees gave way and the world tilted, turned gray, and then black.

Chapter 14

He had been in her house. Donavan Freaking Beecher had been in Joselyn's house.

Pacing back and forth, weapon still in his hand, River glanced over at Joselyn's still body as she lay on his bed. Striding over, he touched her wrist and found her pulse still strongly beating. The steely jaws of the vise constricting his heart loosened marginally allowing him to take a deep breath. Letting it out slowly, he forced himself to stay calm. Feeling a bit more in control, he glanced at the clock and cursed. Where was Bull? It had already been fifteen minutes since Joselyn's scream sent him sprinting up the stairs to find her staring at her destroyed bed. Something in her had snapped, and he prayed she wasn't broken completely. She couldn't be. No, his Joselyn was much too strong to let this destroy her. She was overloaded. She would be okay. She had to be okay.

A loud banging sounded on the door downstairs. "River! Open up; it's Bull."

"Thank God," River breathed as he holstered his weapon and bolted down the stairs. Disengaging the alarm, he threw the door open and stepped out of the way.

Bull entered the foyer. "EMS is right behind me. Have you secured the house?"

River shook his head. "I've been standing guard

over Joselyn." He glanced back up the stairs with longing. He needed to get back to her.

"Go ahead. I'll take care of everything."

River threw Bull a grateful look and raced back to his bedroom. Dropping to his knees beside her, he took her hand and held it in his. Placing a kiss on her fingers, he whispered, "Come on honey, time to wake up for a minute. Let me know you're okay. Please, Joselyn, open your eyes. You're scaring me." He rubbed her cold fingers with his hands.

A woman wearing the navy blue uniform of EMS appeared in the doorway. Taking in the scene, she briskly walked to Joselyn and began to examine her. "What happened?"

Quickly, he ran through the events. She nodded. "Did she hit her head when she fell?"

He shook his head. "I caught her." He stood and raked his fingers through his dark hair. "Will she be okay?"

A second technician stepped into the room carrying a black bag. Sitting it on the edge of the bed, he pulled out a blood pressure sleeve and stethoscope. "Let us finish the exam," she said not unkindly. "It'll take a few minutes. We'll let you know as soon as we are done."

A movement caught his attention, and he glanced over to see Bull standing in the doorway motioning for River. "I'll be right outside if you need me," he said with one more look at Joselyn before joining his friend in the hallway.

Bull wasted no time getting right to the point.

"We've checked the house from top to bottom. There's no sign of forced entry, and all the doors and windows are locked. Was the system armed when you got here?"

He thought for a moment. "I think so. She was already in the house by the time I got there. I know it was armed when we left because I double checked everything. "

"Yeah, I figured as much. You wouldn't let your security instincts lapse; especially not when it involves someone you care about. I'll call the monitoring service and see what they have to say." He lifted a chin toward the doorway. "How is she?"

River glanced back. "I don't know. She's been under a lot of stress lately." He didn't mention his part in adding to her distress.

Bull clasped him on the shoulder. "I'm sure she'll be fine." Barking orders to another officer, he tossed River a chin lift. "Let me know," he said as he rushed downstairs.

"Maddox?"

Relief flew through him as he heard her voice. Hurrying back into his bedroom, he sat on the side of the bed next to her. Pushing a strand of honeyed silk from her face, he smiled. "Hey there. How are you feeling?"

She blinked, and her lip trembled. "He was in my house, in my bedroom."

"I know. Try to stay calm. Bull is here with several officers. You're completely safe." He glanced at the technicians. "Is she okay?"

They were packing the equipment back into its case. "She's fine. Her blood pressure is a little low but rising to normal levels. I advise seeing her doctor to rule out any other issues to be safe." She patted Joselyn's hand, "I hope you feel better. Try to keep the stress down." She gave River another smile and followed her partner out the door.

Joselyn chuckled, but the amusement didn't reach her eyes. "Avoid stress. Wow, they aren't asking for much."

He hated the tension making her eyes bleak and her lips pinch. Reaching out, he smoothed the lines gently with his thumb. "I'm sorry. So damn sorry."

Her eyebrows shot up. "What are you apologizing for?"

He drew in a deep breath and let it go slowly. "I failed you. I swore I would keep you safe and look what happened."

Joselyn searched his face. With a frown, she struggled to a sitting position. "No, you didn't."

Gently he helped her and stuffed his pillow behind her back. "Yes, I did. He got into your house. I was so far into my head; I didn't even check the house like I normally do. What if he had been waiting?"

Once she was comfortable, she pulled him until he sat next to her. Outside the room, he could hear the police as they continued to talk, but his attention was solely on her.

"If he had been waiting, then you would have taken care of him. Maddox, this is not your fault. We both thought the house was safe. There was no reason not to. You made this place a fortress, but he is determined. He figured out a way to get in. I think he came in because we weren't home. I don't think he would chance it with you here, so you're keeping me safe. You, not my house, or even the alarm. It's you."

He wasn't ready for her to forgive him yet. Shaking his head, he started to speak only to have her press her fingers to his lips.

"*Shhh.* Listen to me. You have done everything you can." When he began to protest, she added more forcefully, "Yes, you have. Did he get in? Yes. Did he get to me? No. I'm still here... with you. I'm still safe... with you. He may have found a way in, but he didn't get to me which is more important. So don't beat yourself up here."

He sighed heavily. "When I think what he did, what he could do."

"But he didn't."

"He could have."

"But he didn't, Maddox."

He gazed into her eyes and his heart almost exploded from the raw emotions floating there. Closing his eyes, he murmured, "I'll do better."

She growled and sandwiched his face between her hands. "You're doing fine. I don't like this side of you. I need my hero back. I'll even take the Frost Giant, but this uncertain, self-loathing man has to go. You're a damned SEAL. Buck up, buttercup."

One side lifted into a grin. "I'll let you get by with that but only because you've been through a lot." He kissed her forehead gently. "You cursed again."

"Yeah, I seem to do that a lot around you."

A knock sounded on the door casing. Bull stood in the doorway looking at them expectantly. River stood and reluctantly let her hand go. "Yeah?"

"I talked to the monitoring company. According to their records, Joselyn's code was entered at twenty-one twenty-two last night."

"It's impossible. I was still in Atlanta yesterday."

Bull nodded. "Yeah, we know. But it gave us a time to start searching your security footage." He glanced at River. "You're not going to like this. Come downstairs and take a look."

Joselyn threw her feet over the edge of the bed.

"Whoa. Hang on a minute. Where do you think you're going?" River grabbed her arm as she began to stand.

"I'm going to go see."

He shook his head. "I don't think it's a good idea. You were out cold a few minutes ago. The paramedics said you needed to rest and not get any more stressed."

"I'm beginning to think 'I don't think it's a good idea' is your favorite thing to say to me. Look, I'll be more stressed if I don't know what's going on. Maddox, you should be able to recognize when you've lost an argument with me by now." She walked toward the door. "This is still my house, and I have a right to know what is going on here."

Bull chuckled but stepped out of the way. River tossed him a glare but skulked out the room behind Joselyn's rigid back. With a grand gesture wave, Bull motioned them to the stairs. "After you." The three of them entered her study where several officers stood staring at the security camera screens. One policeman sat at the little table underneath, controlling the view with clicks of a mouse button.

"Okay, Johnson, show them what we found from last night."

A few clicks and a picture zoomed from the bottom to fill the screen. It showed a figure dressed in dark clothes wearing a hoodie and a baseball cap pulled down low underneath. A slight hazing created an ethereal atmosphere as rain slowly turned the gray garment a darker charcoal. He stood before one of her rose bushes in the garden, his hand outstretched toward one of the blossoms. With a click, the footage resumed motion. They watched as he plucked petal after petal and placed them into his other gloved hand cradled against his stomach. Beside him, Joselyn gasped. "Mom's roses," she whispered with a hitch in her voice. "He got the petals from my mom's climbing roses."

The distress in her voice cut into River. Gently, he pulled her closer to him and wrapped his arm around her back to rest on her hip. There were no words to ease the betrayal at seeing her mother's roses defiled in such a manner. It made him sick.

He turned back to the screen as another image filled it. This time, the man stood at the back door, silhouetted in the glare of the motion-sensitive floodlight placed there. He drew out a key from his pocket and pushed it into the lock. With a twist, he entered the door turned to the right, and poked at the wall. Leaving the door open, he moved deeper into her house. The stamp on the bottom right of the screen displayed the time - 21:22.

"Son of a..." River swore. "He has a key and the alarm code. How the hell is that possible?"

"I said you weren't going to like it. He stayed in the house for seventeen minutes. The camera picks him up leaving again." He tapped Johnson's shoulder, and the screen showed the man leaving, pulling the door closed once again. "According to the logs, he didn't re-arm the system."

"I didn't realize the system wasn't on. I was..." she glanced at River, her face turning bright pink. "I was so exhausted I didn't even think about it at the time. But now I'm unsure if it beeped at me when I opened the door."

"And I was getting the bags out of the truck. I thought you had done it."

He felt like an idiot. No, strike that, an incompetent idiot. He had let his pigheadedness get in the way of his duty, and it could have cost Joselyn her life. He stared off into space.

"Stop it."

He jerked his head around to see her staring at him with a frown on her face. "What?"

"Stop beating yourself over this. It's not your fault. Cheebus, Maddox, you've done everything you can here. He got in the house one time. Determined people will find a way."

Bull coughed. "Ah, actually, he's been in your house more than once."

"What?" Both of them exclaimed at the same time.

"Go ahead," Bull told the tech.

A few clicks and several pictures filled the screen.

"I've been scanning the feed all the way back to the installation. He's visited the location six times but only entered the house four," Johnson intoned. Pointing to the screen, he continued. "Here, here, here and yesterday. Each time you were out of the house. I think it's probably because Mr. Benson was in residence."

"What is he carrying?" One of the officers pointed to the first picture showing the intruder leaving the back door with something over his arm.

Johnson zoomed in. "Looks like some sort of garment." He fiddled with the controls until the picture sharpened and brightened. "I'm not sure. Something... dark? The fog is distorting the image slightly, but it looks like a coat or a maybe a dress."

Joselyn gasped, whirled around, pushed past the others and out of the room.

"Joselyn!" River tore after her as she ran up the stairs. He followed her into her bedroom and through to the closet. She pushed shirts, slacks, and dresses aside mumbling, "I know it's here. It has to be here."

"What, honey? What are you looking for?'

She finished her search and turned to face him.

Slowly she dropped to the carpeted floor and drew her knees to her chest, wrapping her arms around her legs. "It's gone. He's got it."

Sitting beside her, he slid his arm around her shoulders. "What's gone? What does he have?"

She looked at him with fear and tears swimming in her eyes. His heart shattered at the expression of complete hopelessness. He never wanted to see that look on her face again. "My dress. The purple one from the video. The one I wore on Douglas McClane's verdict day."

River's eyes hardened, and he swore. It didn't escape his notice she was too upset to reprimand him for his language. Pulling her into his lap, he wrapped his arms around her shaking body and ran his hand over her arm. He rocked her gently as he felt his shirt dampen with her tears. Each wrenching sob tore out a piece of his heart. Looking up, he saw Bull standing in the doorway watching them with an inscrutable look on his face.

"I've had enough of this insanity, Bull. This pervert has messed with us for the last time."

Bull nodded. "I agree. It's time to finish this. What do you suggest?"

River looked down at the beauty nestled against his chest and pressed his lips to her temple. "I need to get her out of here. I'm taking her someplace I can control; where I know he can't get to her, Somewhere he doesn't know anything about. I'm taking her home."

Chapter 15

"Oh, baby, why didn't you tell me what was going on? You know how worried we were when that horrible man was stalking you."

Joselyn grimaced. "Which is why I didn't tell you, Mom. I didn't want you to be worried. You have enough going on. How is Aunt Laura?"

"Better. This round of chemotherapy has knocked her down. She's taking a nap at the moment. Don't think I don't realize you're trying to change the subject. I want to know what the police are doing to keep you safe."

"Everything they can. I'm fine, I promise. Maddox is taking good care of me."

Her mother's voice lightened, and Joselyn could almost hear the teasing smile behind it. "Tell me more about this bodyguard of yours who is taking such good care of my baby."

Joselyn glanced over at him as he navigated the two-lane Mississippi road. Gazing ahead intently, she noticed the periodic flick of his eyes on the mirrors to ensure they were not being followed. Reaching over, she squeezed his hand firmly and got a smile in return. Turning his head, he winked at her before returning his attention to the road ahead.

"He's former military, a SEAL, and extremely capable of taking care of any situation which may arise."

"And?"

"And what, Mom?"

Her mother huffed. "And what does he look like? Is there a spark between you? There must be because your voice gets all breathy when you say his name. *Maaddoox*."

"Mom!" Joselyn squeaked. Shooting a look over at him to see if he heard, she saw one corner of his mouth tug upwards ever so slightly. *Lord, open the ground right here and swallow her whole!*

"Well?"

Joselyn chose her words carefully. "He's my bodyguard. He's a professional."

Her mother laughed. "I see. He's a professional. Joselyn Annalisa Kendrik, you can't hide from me. You like him. You like him a lot."

Pulling her hand out of his, she turned toward the door. Cupping her hand around the mouthpiece, she whispered, "Yeah. I do." She wasn't about to explain to her mother exactly how much she liked Maddox Benson, especially not with him sitting a couple of feet away. She was head over heels in love with him. "Look, I'll call you later, and we can talk more. I gave you his Aunt and Uncle's telephone number. Maddox doesn't want to take a chance in case someone may be able to track me using the GPS on my cell, so I'm going to be offline. If you need me, call them. Okay?"

"Alright baby. You be careful. And Joselyn?"

"Yes, Mom?"

"When this is over, I expect to meet your capable bodyguard. Do you understand me?"

She couldn't hide the grin. "Yes, Ma'am. Love you. Give Aunt Laura my love please."

"I will. Love you, too."

The line went dead, and she immediately turned her cell off. Stuffing it into her purse, she relaxed back into the soft leather cushions of the truck seats. "So, tell me about this farm we're going to. Aren't you afraid of bringing trouble to their door?"

"Nope. Nobody knows about the farm. However, if trouble comes, they will be sorry. Uncle Aaron is ex-military. He was a Green Beret, and there's nobody I'd rather have my six besides my team. He may be older and a little slower, but he's still deadly. The rumor in the family is he could go into the woods with a rifle and three bullets and come out with a buck, six rabbits and still have one bullet left." Maddox chuckled softly. "He's the reason I decided to go into the SEALs."

She nodded slowly as she absorbed the information. "So, answer this for me. I saw *Black Hawk Down* which had Delta Force in it. I know both Delta and Green Berets are special forces for the Army sort of like SEALs are for the Navy. What is the difference between Delta and Green Beret? Aren't they the same thing?

He hesitated as he changed lanes and slowed. Checking the mirrors, he turned the truck onto a dirt road. "No, they aren't the same. Until a few years ago, nobody even knew Delta Force existed. They deal mostly with black ops. It's so hushed, if one of them dies, they aren't even acknowledged as being in Delta Force. Green Berets is white ops and well known. You want something done, call the Green Berets. You want it done, and nobody ever knows there was a problem much less a solution, call Delta."

A shiver crept up her back. "And the SEALs?"

His gaze found hers and smirked. "SEALs are badasses who get the job done. Period. We don't care about the color of the op. We go in, get it done, and go home." He patted her hand. He slowed and drove over the cattle guard and around the driveway. On both sides, dogs barked and ran alongside. Cresting a small hill, he finally stopped in front of a large house beside an old beat up truck.

Joselyn gazed at the building. It was exactly how she thought a farm should look. There was a two-storey house made of white clapboard with a huge wraparound porch sitting in the midst of a huge yard with several tall trees shading the lawn. To one side, she saw a large barn and several smaller buildings including a chicken coop and storage shed. An older faded green tractor rested underneath. Behind the house, she could just see another, larger shed peeking out with some sort of large vehicle underneath. Even though the closed windows, she could hear the sounds of horses, cows and other animals nearby. Rail fences weathered to gray encased the perimeter of the property as far as the eye could see. Craning her neck, she caught the sight of a sea of gently waving grass in the pasture. Shadows lengthen as the sun sank behind the barn. She smiled wistfully. Norman Rockwell would have a field day here.

As Maddox got out before going around and opening her door, an older couple stood up from a pair of matching rocking chairs and peered at the truck expectantly. Huge grins erupted on their faces when they recognized him.

"Maddox!" The woman moved quickly down the steps and reached up to embrace him. Wearing a pair of worn denim jeans and an old blue checked shirt she was still much shorter than him, even with a pair of muddy boots on her feet. Her dark brown eyes sparkled as Maddox dropped a kiss onto her forehead. Standing back, she held his hands and tsked. "We haven't heard from you in so long. Your mother is going to be over the moon."

Once his aunt released him, he turned to his uncle and clasped hands. With a tug, the huge man pulled his nephew into an embrace before slapping him soundly on the back. "Good to see you, Son," he boomed. "It's been much too long since you last came to visit." He tousled Maddox's hair like he was a small child. "Getting a little shaggy there. You forget your barber's address?"

He chuckled. "The SEALs prefer it; longer hair helps us blend in. The last thing we need while in another country is to stand out and look like military. However, you're right; it's gotten a little too long. I'll get it cut soon."

Joselyn stood quietly by the front of the truck and watched the family reunion unfold. She could see a strong resemblance between Maddox and his uncle. Both men were tall and soundly built. Though Maddox's was still black and longer, his uncle's hair was much short and shot through with silver. They both had the same smile, same nose, and the exact same ice blue eyes. Looking at his uncle, Joselyn felt as if she was getting a glimpse of Maddox in another thirty years.

As if he suddenly remembered she was there, Maddox motioned for her to join him. His aunt's eyebrows raised as she looked Joselyn over." Uncle Aaron, Aunt Celia, this is Joselyn Kendrik."

Feeling a bit awkward, Joselyn gave them both a brilliant smile and held out her hand. "Hello," she stated. "I'm very pleased to meet you. You have a lovely place here."

Celia clucked her tongue and pulled her into her arms. "None of that handshake stuff with family." Hugging her tight, Celia let her go and looked her over again. "Really happy to meet you. Maddox hasn't brought home a friend before." Wrapping an arm around Joselyn's waist, she pulled her toward the porch. "Come have a seat. Supper will be ready in an hour, so let's relax a bit and get to know each other. I made a pot roast tonight. Good time to visit because I know how much you like it, Maddox. "Helping Joselyn to a rocker, she asked them, "Tea or lemonade?"

"Tea, please," she said politely.

"Same," Maddox agreed.

Celia nodded and disappeared into the house. She emerged a few moments later with a tray carrying several ice-filled glasses and a pitcher of tea. Behind her, a man and a woman followed.

A genuine smile lit Maddox's face. "Shaun! Hannah!" He stood and hugged them both. "I didn't know you were home. Last I heard it would be a few weeks yet. Where's your rig?" He held Hannah at arm's length. "You look stunning." He touched her rounded stomach. "Congratulations."

Hannah looked at her husband. "The RV is in the back, out of the way. I've had some pretty gnarly morning sickness which lasts all day so the company I obtain my contracts through let me out early with no repercussions. They had another nurse ready to begin." She lifted her shoulders in a shrug. "So here we are."

Joselyn watched the two cousins interact. They seemed to be so close, and it was the first time she had ever seen Maddox truly relax. Rocking the chair with her feet, she melted into the cushion and turned her gaze to the scenery. It wasn't exactly quiet, but it was peaceful. She sighed happily. Even if she hadn't been forced from her home by a crazed maniac, this was a good idea. Until this moment, she hadn't realized how mentally exhausted she had become.

Her attention was drawn back to the discussion as Maddox introduced her to Shaun and Hannah. Afterward, everyone slipped into easy conversations about the farm. When there was a lull, Aaron looked at Maddox in the same strange manner as most parents when they knew something was going on. Finally, he spoke. "Not that we're not glad to see you, but I'm surprised you didn't tell us you were coming. I talked to Sarah yesterday, and she didn't say anything about you being on leave."

Maddox swept his hand through his hair. "Ah, yeah, well, about that. Mom doesn't know I'm here and I'm not on leave."

"Boy, if you went AWOL..." Aaron jumped to his feet.

Maddox stopped him with a slash of his hand. "I'm not AWOL. I retired. Last month."

The silence of shock filled the air. Suddenly, everyone began talking at once.

Maddox halted the confusion with a raised hand. "One minute, please, and I'll explain. I didn't tell anyone I was retiring because I didn't know I was going to until the last minute. I had decided to re-up again for another tour, but when I got my reenlistment papers, CO told me they were going to move me to a desk job. I'm still in good shape, and I still meet the requirements, but with new blood coming in, they were going to put me into a position where they could, as they said, 'utilize my vast experience more logistically.' I'm not cut out to be a desk jockey, so I opted out. Twenty years is enough for me if he wasn't going to put me back on my team. It happened quickly; I decided while standing there in his office with the papers in my hand. Once I was out, it hit me I had no real plans where my future was concerned. I figured I would see Mom for a bit and maybe help out on the farm here for the summer. Well, it was my original intention, but you know how those can go." He looked at Joselyn and winked.

"Hmmm," Hannah hummed knowingly.

Maddox laughed. "Not what you think." He

proceeded to tell them about the telephone call from Bull, driving to New Orleans and everything that had happened since. When he was done, Aaron whistled.

"I'm glad you brought her here. Between the three of us, we can keep a good eye on her."

Joselyn's brow wrinkled. "Aren't you concerned about Celia and Hannah?"

Aaron chuckled. "If anybody is foolish enough to come on this farm thinking he's going to mess with my ladies, he's going to be hopping out of here with a few pounds of lead in his butt. You don't worry about us, Joselyn. We take care of our own, and now that includes you as well."

Celia chose that moment to stand and clap her hands together. "Alright, enough jabbering for now. Dinner should be ready, and I don't want to feed you a stringy, dry roast so let's get to it." She stopped and patted Joselyn's arm. "Don't you worry none at all, honey. Everything will be fine."

Joselyn smiled gratefully. "Thank you so much for the warm welcome."

Celia snorted. "Think nothing of it."

Joselyn followed them into the house. For the first time, she felt as if a weight had lifted off her shoulders and she could relax. As if reading her thoughts, Maddox leaned over and pressed his lips to her temple.

"You're safe, honey, just like I promised you."

Chapter 16

*R*iver sat back on his haunches, turned on the hose, and splashed water onto his face and head. Standing, he turned off the spigot, pulled off his shirt and wiped the rivulets of water from his shoulders and chest. With a casual thrust of his fingers through his hair to push it back off his face, he mopped it with his shirt and tossed the damp material onto his shoulder. He retrieved the shovel from where he had left it and quickly placed it back into the storage shed. Rounding the corner, he stopped in his tracks and searched for Joselyn. He relaxed to find her sitting on the porch, a large bowl of dried peanuts in her lap and a brilliant smile on her face. Reaching the porch, he stopped in front of her, leaned against the rail and watched her. She had easily settled into life on the farm.

His heart lurched when heard her laughing at something Hannah said. Again, he was amazed at how quickly he had fallen for this beautiful woman. Seeing her there so comfortable and carefree eased his tension. He longed to see her like this rather than fear drawing her face into harder lines. She looked into the bowl, picked a plump brown pod, popped it open and removed the nuts. The discarded hulls were dropped into a bin at her feet. Glancing up, she noticed him watching her and she averted her gaze as her face turned a beautiful shade of pink.

"Hey." She tossed her head, sending a few tendrils of hair out of her eyes. "Celia is going to teach me how to make peanut butter."

River grinned. "She always made the best. I can remember many hours spent shelling peanuts for her."

"And eating them. I swear, between you and Shaun, I'd give you enough peanuts to make a dozen jars but somehow only got seven or eight. "

Laughter filled the air. "True, but we were careful not to eat too many. We sure didn't want a stomach ache knowing you were going to make cookies with it later."

She pursed her lips. "Which reminds me. I need to make some cookies and take them over to Lenora Ellis' house tomorrow. The ladies' auxiliary is feeding the family while she's recovering from surgery."

"Please tell me you're going to give Joselyn your recipe." He leaned over the rail. "I've been trying for years to get it out of you. Nobody knows the secret of your cookies, but everyone agrees they are the best."

"You know the rule, Maddox. Only the women folk of the family get the recipe." She flashed him a knowing smile. "Joselyn is sweet as apple pie, but she's not family. Yet."

The implied meaning hung in the air, catching Joselyn as she was taking a drink of tea. She coughed on the drink and Hannah reached over, pounding her on the back while Joselyn's eyes watered. "Drink it don't breath it, hon," Hannah said with a laugh.

"So, are you through already?" Celia queried.

River noticed how she steered the attention away from the loaded statement and chuckled. That was Aunt Celia for you - zing one in one second and take the sting out the next. He nodded. "Yep. Mucking out a stable goes a lot faster when you aren't trying to find a dozen reasons to avoid it. Shaun went to check on Uncle Aaron." He looked at the darkening sky. "Looks like rain this afternoon so Shaun figured he'd help him finish checking on the cows."

He hopped up on the porch, reached into Joselyn's bowl and stole a handful of nuts. She yelled at him then slapped his arm playfully. Making a face, she drew back and waved her hand in front of her face. "Shoo! You're rank!"

He shrugged. "There's a reason it's called mucking. The stuff in the stalls is half straw and half crap. And when I say crap, I mean crap. Always amazed me how sweet smelling hay and grass turned so smelly in a horse's stomach. You know, I played around with the idea of becoming a veterinarian once. I figured curiosity over a cow's digestive tract wasn't a good reason to spend ten years in school though."

"Go on and get a shower. You're not fit for mixed company," his aunt said. "Put your dirty clothes in the hamper in the hall and not the one in the bathroom. I wash work clothes separate."

"I remember," he said and dropped a kiss on his aunt's cheek. Giving Joselyn a wink, he toed off his work boots and entered the house in his sock-covered feet.

Last night, after dinner was finished, River and Joselyn had told them more about the stalker who was after her, including his gifts and the way he had invaded her home. Predictably, they were outraged and reaffirmed their welcome to the farm. She could stay as long as she liked and that made Joselyn visibly relax. This morning, over coffee, the three men discussed strategy and security measures. Once plans were made, the three disappeared to do morning chores. After all, this was a working farm. That meant, if you ate at the table, you worked. Neither River nor Joselyn would be able to laze around all day doing nothing. Even Hannah, in her delicate state, was given a few easy things to do. It was decided River would complete the chores closer to the house and barn. There was no way Donavan Beecher could find them, but River wasn't taking any chances. Until Bull called with the all clear, he was sticking to Joselyn like glue.

Showered and changed, River rejoined them on the porch. The pile of hulls had gotten noticeably larger, and the number of bowls to be shelled were much smaller. Reaching over, he grabbed another handful and tossed them into his mouth. Aunt Celia clucked in displeasure.

River sat in the swing and watched the ladies as they talked and worked. It was so relaxing here; he had forgotten how wonderful the farm was. Memories of countless summers flashed through his mind. It had been the perfect place to grow up, and he wanted the same sort of life for his children one day.

He froze in shock. Where had that thought come from? River shook his head to clear it. It was too early even to entertain anything like futures with children and maybe a sweet but feisty blonde-haired beauty at his side. He glanced at Joselyn again and caught her watching him through her thick lashes. She looked so beautiful; it made his heartache. When she let him kiss her, he felt as if he had the world in his pocket. When she let him hold and comfort her, there was nothing he couldn't do. She mattered to him. He snorted to himself. Who was he kidding? She more than merely mattered. He had fallen for her. He winked at her, and she turned back to the peanuts. Yeah, they needed to talk. Sooner rather than later.

"Oh, Maddox, while I'm thinking about it. My knives could use sharpening. Aaron doesn't do as well as you. Would you mind?"

He shook his head. "I don't mind one bit," he told Celia. Getting to his feet, he retrieved the block containing her kitchen knives along with a whetstone, hand towel and a bit of oil. Taking them back to the porch, he sat on the swing and went to work. Joselyn nudged the table she was using toward him.

"We can share," she said.

The conversation continued in a low hum as they all worked. Presently, Aaron and Shaun joined them. With a kiss, Hannah sent her husband for a shower, and Uncle Aaron stood in the yard watching the gathering clouds. "Going to be a bad one," he said nonchalantly. I'll go check the lamps in the house and shelter in case we lose power later." Climbing the steps, he disappeared into the house.

Yep, at this moment, River remembered every single reason why he loved this place but more importantly, he saw the best reason to want something like this in his future. The reason was sitting next to him, her cheeks flushed and her caramel eyes shining full of happiness as she shelled peanuts into a bowl.

Chapter 17

Joselyn settled into farm life with more ease than she would have thought possible. Waking early to help feed the animals and work in the garden took some getting used to, but after two weeks, it had become second nature. Placing the basket of tomatoes she had picked on the counter, she called out a good morning to the ladies and went into the basement to retrieve a box of jars. Today they would make canned tomato relish (or chow-chow as Celia called it) for the winter. Joselyn loved the tangy condiment and was looking forward to learning Celia's special technique in combining tomatoes, peppers, cabbage and assorted seasonings.

Later that afternoon, she was fishing out the last jar from the water bath when she felt eyes on her. Glancing over her shoulder, she grinned at Maddox standing against the wall with his arms crossed over his chest, and a ratty straw hat pulled low over his brow. As was the norm, her breath caught, and her heart stuttered when he flashed a heated gaze her way. Wiping her hands on her apron, she walked over to him and circled his waist with her arms. "Hi."

"Hi back. You look pretty domesticated there."

"I think farm life suits me."

He reached out and twirled a strand of hair falling out of her kerchief around his fingers. His clear blue gaze was full of longing as he watched it slide through his rough hands like silk. "It does suit you." He agreed. "Go for a walk with me?"

She froze. "Detective Jameson called you?"

He shook his head. "I thought you would like to get out a bit. Come on."

"I don't know. There are dishes to do and dinner to start."

"Go on, Joselyn. Hannah and I have this. A little fresh air would do you good," Celia called out. "It's pretty by the pond with all the wildflowers in bloom. Aaron used to take me there all the time for romantic little picnics. The stars are fantastic."

Joselyn snorted. That sounded about right. Celia had been playing matchmaker since the day they arrived. "It's the middle of the afternoon. I don't think we'll see many stars."

Celia shrugged as she wrote out labels for the jars. "Doesn't mean you can't go back when it's dark."

Maddox laughed in the easy way he had adopted over the past few weeks. The vigilant demeanor was still there, but the stressful glare had all but disappeared. She hadn't seen the Frost Giant visage since New Orleans. She liked this version of him even more than the other.

He pulled the tie holding her apron around her waist and tossed it on the counter. "We'll be back in time to help with dinner," he called out. Curling his hand about hers, he tugged her out of the door and down the steps.

They walked together, hand in hand, through the

pasture and into the wood line. Joselyn was happy to be there with him. He made her forget the problems back in New Orleans. Glancing over at him, she marveled again at how deep her feelings had become. In the space of a few weeks, he had changed from the cold Frost Giant to this loving, protective man. Ever since her time in WitSec, she hadn't felt the urge to date very much - she was too busy getting her life in order. It seemed perfect for him to appear when she needed him most, physically and emotionally. Wrapping her hand around his beefy forearm, she pressed her cheek against his shoulder. Even as horrible as the circumstances were which brought them together, there was a silver lining. To have even this small chance at something special with him meant the world to her.

After a few minutes, they emerged from the woods into a little clearing. Scattered about in the knee-high weeds were several piles of large stones bound together with some sort of gray mortar. Leading her over to one, he placed his hands around her waist and gently lifted her to the top. Once she was settled, he jumped up to sit beside her.

His warmth felt good pressed against her side. Seeking more of it, she leaned against him and placed her head on his shoulder. They sat that way for a long while, taking in the serenity of nature and the comfort of being together.

"I love it here. So peaceful and pretty. What are all these blocks? They look like a foundation of some sort. Was there a house here at one time?"

His arm curled around her back until his hand

rested on her hip. Gently running his fingers over the seam on the side of her jeans, he spoke. "In 1842, Jonas Rickers settled here on 480 acres of land he purchased using an inheritance he received from a relative in Europe. He, along with his three sons, two daughters and their families worked this land and made it profitable. Jonas didn't believe in slave labor, so they worked long, hard hours. Then the Civil War broke out. All three of the sons and both sons-in-law went to fight. Some say they all fought for the North and others believe they were split. Either way, he lost two of his sons and both sons-in-law to the hostilities. To add insult to injury, Northern troops razed the farm during the Meridian Campaign in early 1864." He patted the rock they sat upon. "This is all that is left of the original foundation." He motioned toward the trees. "There was a barn over there somewhere. According to family stories, soldiers slept in it one night and burned it down the next. Distraught over losing so much so quickly, Jonas refused to rebuild on the original site. The current house was completed in 1875 right where it sits now." He looked around wistfully. "There's something about the old homestead. I'm not saying it's haunted, but there's an almost reverent quality to the place, a quiet serenity infused here. Sometimes, I would come out here to sit and think about things when I wanted to get away from Shaun for a bit. He could be a real pain at times." He reached down and pulled a stalk of grass and slowly shred it between his beefy fingers. "This is one of my favorite places, and I wanted to share it with you."

Joselyn thought about what he was saying. He brought her to one of his cherished memories and shared it with her. She smiled up at him. "Thank you for bringing me here."

"You're welcome." He pressed his lips to her head in a sweet little kiss.

"Why do you do that?"

He pulled back. "Why do I do what?"

"Kiss my head. I notice you do it all the time now. I was just wondering why."

He drew in a breath and let it go slowly. "I do it because I want to touch you. I want to kiss you and be close to you."

"Then why don't you just kiss me?"

He cupped his hand against her cheek, traced the contour of her jaw and tenderly ran his thumb over her plump lips. His eyes searched hers as he murmured, "Because I don't think I could stop if I ever gave in."

Her breath hitched. Staring into the beautiful blue of his eyes, she whispered, "Do you have to stop?"

Maddox groaned and pressed his forehead against hers. "You tempt me badly and what I want is more than either of us can handle right now. Sweetheart, you're so beautiful, so strong and sexy, I can't think straight around you. The way you look at me with those big brown eyes of yours makes me have thoughts that I promised you I wouldn't act upon. I need to touch and tease and taste you. I want to hear your little moans of happiness as I show you how much I care for you. I want to explore you, learn your body and find out everything about you. I know this sounds Neanderthal, but I want to possess you, care for you, place you up so high on a pedestal nobody can touch you. I want to mark you as mine so nobody ever thinks they can take you away."

She swallowed at his frank admission. "You do?" she squeaked.

He nodded slowly. "So much. Joselyn, I know we haven't known each other for a long time, and many people may say what I feel is a natural progression brought about by my protective instincts, but it's not. What I feel is real, pure and so deep. I swore I wouldn't get involved. I told myself I could remain aloof and not let things get intimate between us, but it's a big lie because I can't do it. I can't be away from you. I wake up in the morning and rush to get things done so I can find you. When I go to sleep at night, the only way I can bear being away from you is knowing you will be in my dreams. You're it for me, Joselyn. You're everything and more." Cupping her face with both hands, he hesitated a second and said the words that rocked her world. "You're mine, sweetheart. Mine to keep, mine to protect, mine to love. I love you, Joselyn."

The tears that spilled down her cheeks were ones of happiness."I think I've been in love with you since the day I first saw you." Joselyn threw her arms around his neck and kissed him.

Maddox stilled a second in shock before taking over. Teasing her mouth gently, she opened to him, and he dived inside to ravage and claim her. Tongues tangling, they pressed close to each other, clinging with abandon as passion flared between them. She moaned, her breath captured by him until they finally broke apart panting.

He drew a ragged breath and cleared his throat, letting her face go reluctantly. "Okay then. "

She laughed softly. "See, you can stop." Her fingers slid under his tee-shirt and caressed his warm skin lightly. Tracing the unseen scars on his chest, she whispered, "I may not be able to."

He groaned and captured her wandering hand with his. "Darlin', you aren't making this easy. I'm already on edge, so please don't poke the beast. "

"Oh," she whispered as her face turned red.

"Yeah, oh." He nuzzled against her neck. "I made you a promise, and I'm not going to break it, no matter how much my libido is screaming otherwise."

"I know most people in today's age would think it's silly to want to wait. The whole white wedding dress and all. I mean, I know women still wear white, regardless but..." she started.

He pressed his hand against her back and gently caressed her. "No, it's not. It's special, and I'm so proud of you for standing up for what you believe in. We can wait. We will wait because I'm not going to let either of us destroy a promise to your father and yourself. It's been your dream for so long, and I refuse to take it away - not even if we both want it so bad we can't think straight. I'll be strong enough for us both. But Joselyn, when this thing with Beecher is over, we need to have a long talk about the future. We need to make some decisions because I'll wait for now. However, you must understand something. I intend to make you mine." Lifting her hand to his lips, he pressed a kiss to the back of her hand. "One day, I'll replace this ring with one of my own."

Joselyn nodded, too overwhelmed with emotions to speak. Unless she was mistaken, he was all but proposing to her. She glanced at the simple silver ring her father had given her. Tears welled in her eyes at the sweet gesture from Maddox. He understood her better than anyone else ever could, and she loved him all the more for it. She would always remember this moment as the happiest of her life. Right here, right now, in the safety of Maddox's arms, she forgot about Donavan Beecher and basked in the knowledge that Maddox loved her.

They sat together for a while, watching the windblown branches sway, and talked about nothing in particular. Joselyn enjoyed being in Maddox's company, and he did in hers as well. After a while, he stood and tugged her off the rocks and into his arms. They shared another passionate kiss before returning to the farmhouse.

"Celia will be thrilled, you know," Joselyn remarked as they walked arm in arm. "She has been trying to sell me on you since the day we got here. I didn't have the heart to tell her it was useless because I had already fallen."

"Aunt Celia means well. She fancies herself a matchmaker." He hugged her tighter to his side. "I'm sure she'll take credit for us."

"Hmmm," she agreed. "Let her. I don't care one way or the other. As long as I have you in my life, I'm happy. Right here is where I need to be."

"Forever," he whispered and kissed her head again.

They climbed the little hill in the pasture and stopped at the top. "Company," he said. "Stay close to me. It's probably a neighbor but better safe than sorry." He popped the lock on his holster so he could remove his weapon quickly if needed. "If I tell you to run, you run to the barn and into the storm cellar underneath. Lock the door and stay out of sight until I come get you."

"Okay," she said with a nod of her head and dug her fingers into his arm. "What about Celia and Hannah?"

"We'll take care of them. Calm down, honey. I'm sure it's nothing."

Joselyn didn't answer as they made their way to the house. Walking through the little gate, Maddox suddenly relaxed and replaced his sidearm in his holster. "It's good," he said, rushing up the steps. "Mom! I didn't know you were coming."

An older woman, who had to be in her late sixties stood on the porch talking to Aaron and Celia. Joselyn could see the family resemblance. Her short, silver hair was done into a fashionable bob causing her pale blue eyes to pop. Dressed in jeans and a short sleeve shirt, she threw her arms around Maddox and hugged him tightly. "There's my baby boy! I thought I was going to have to go looking for you."

"Nah, we were taking a little walk." Taking a step back, he motioned to Joselyn. "Mom, I want you to meet Joselyn Kendrik. Joselyn, this is my mother, Sarah Benson."

Joselyn held her hand out. "So pleased to meet you," she said.

Sarah looked her over a second and broke into a broad grin. Grabbing her hand, she pulled her into a tight hug. "I'm so happy to meet you, dear. I've heard so much about you." She glared at Maddox. "Mostly from Celia."

Beside her, Maddox coughed and mumbled something inaudible as Joselyn blushed slightly. "Thank you," she managed to say.

Sarah let her go and dropped into a rocking chair. "Have a seat. I want to get to know all about you, Joselyn. Celia tells me you two are thick as thieves. She also told me about your problem. I know our Maddox is taking care of everything."

Joselyn nodded. "He takes excellent care of me. You have raised a wonderful son, Ms. Benson."

"None of that 'Ms. Benson' stuff; call me Sarah. Thank you but I have to admit most of the credit for this one goes to Aaron and Celia. Sometimes it does take a village."

The topic changed to family, mostly Sarah's other children and grandchildren. Maddox sat on a bench and pulled Joselyn into his lap. She colored as everyone's eyes widened at this new display of affection but she didn't mind. He pulled her back against him and wrapped his arms around her waist. It felt special and right. He was following through on his vow to make her his, and it thrilled her. At this moment she knew what it meant to be in Heaven because surely this was it, in Maddox's arms.

Chapter 18

"Good evening, Sam."

The guard started slightly and looked sheepishly from the novel he was reading. "Oh, hello, Artemis. Sorry, I didn't see you." He lifted the book. "Joselyn Chamber's new one came out this morning." He stuck a piece of paper between the pages and closed it. "I love all her books, but this one is particularly good."

Artemis dropped a cup of coffee onto the window sill of the guard house and motioned to it. "Black as my soul, just the way you like it." He lifted his chin toward the book resting on the table. "It's so unusual in today's age to see someone still enjoying a hardback. I thought everyone had one of those electronic things with a thousand books at a time."

Sam took a sip, "Mmm good coffee and exactly what I needed." He chuckled. "My wife loves e-readers. She's an avid reader but dislikes carrying books around. She said when she was younger, she always kept one or two paperbacks in her purse and hated the bulky weight. Now she has no less than four e-readers scattered around the house." He shook his head. "Give me the smell of paper and being able to feel the book in my hands any day. Not to mention, you can't get autographs on electronic readers." He picked up the hardback again and shook it carefully. "I'm hoping to get this one signed soon."

"May I?" Artemis motioned toward the book.

Sam handed it to him and watched him look the volume over, turning it in his hands and reading the back dust cover. Opening the front, he read the front blurb and nodded his head. Handing it back, he smiled. "Looks like a good one. I'm usually more into the classics, but there's nothing wrong with a good murder mystery. I'm not sure I've heard of this writer before. Is she new?"

Sam placed the book carefully on the little table housing the two gate screens and his keys. "She's still new but extremely good. This is her third one and so far, the best. I understand the fourth in this series is set to come out this fall." He glanced around and leaned in toward the man. "She lives right in this community! Can you believe it?"

With a widening of his eyes, Artemis looked around. "Really? Do we have a famous author living here? Where?"

Sam sat back. "I can't say, privacy and all. She's out of town for a while, but when she gets back, I'm going to ask her to sign this copy." He placed a hand on the book. "I highly recommend trying one of hers. I have a paperback at home of the second in this series. If you like, I'll bring it so you can read it."

The man stared thoughtfully at the book, chewing his lip. He seemed lost in his thoughts, so Sam nudged Artemis' hand where it sat on the guardhouse window sill. Artemis glared at him a split second and pulled his hand back. Smoothing his face, he smiled again. "Excuse me for my inattention, Sam. Blanked out there for a minute. You were saying?"

"I asked if you would like to read one of Ms. Chamber's books? I have a paperback copy at home.

"I would appreciate it, Sam. Thank you. If I like her, do you think I could get her autograph as well?"

Sam lifted his shoulders in a shrug. "I suppose you could leave a book with me and I'll get her to sign it when she gets back. I'm betting you'll like her. She is a bestselling author on several lists. Her stories are awesome."

"Hmmm," Artemis murmured. "There's a problem. You see, the Progues will be home soon, and I'll be leaving the area. Unless she's coming home in the next couple of days, I'll miss my opportunity. What a shame. Even if I wasn't a fan right now, I hate missing out on an opportunity to get a signed copy of a bestselling author's book. You have no idea when she'll return home?"

Sam shook his head and looked at the book again. With a slight incline of his head, he made a decision and leaned out the window. "Alright, I'll tell you what I'll do. There's a box that came today for her. It'll be forwarded to her tomorrow morning. If you get a copy of her book and give it to me, I'll slide it in with the other stuff and ship it out to her. I'm sure she'll be happy to sign it and return it before you leave," he said conspiratorially. "She loves her fans and will normally do anything to make them happy."

He grinned. "Fantastic! I'll get a copy and bring it back. Thanks a lot, Sam. I appreciate it." He glanced at the boxes sitting at Sam's feet and nodded. "You have no idea how much I appreciate this."

Well, that had gone better than he thought it would.

When the man known as Artemis King had first spied Sam reading Joselyn's latest book, he had hoped to gain some insight into how long before his Little Rose returned to her garden. Glancing over at the house where she lived he paused on the Progues porch and let his thoughts run. It was a stroke of pure luck that a connection to her present location was sitting in the pile of boxes in the guard shack. He rubbed his bottom lip with a perfectly manicured thumbnail and thought. How would he use this information? Could he lure her home early? Some emergency with her house may do it. He shook his head. With the police watching her house so carefully, he didn't dare return there although he longed to. A glower marred his face as he recalled the narrow miss a few days ago. He had almost been caught in her backyard. It was pure fortune he was able to climb the pergola in the garden and jump over her wall. Reaching down, he scratched the cut the spike had left on his ankle. The fact he had escaped with only a tiny scratch cemented in his mind the powers-that-be wanted him to obtain her. There could be no other reason.

He stared at the guard shack and tapped his lip slowly. Making friends with the outgoing security guard had been another stroke of pure genius. The bumbling oaf hadn't realized how much information he had fed him concerning The Rose's actions and whereabouts. Pulling his key out of his pocket, he let himself into the Progues house. Good thing too. Once that soldier had whisked her off a few weeks ago, the calendar he had downloaded from her cell phone had become worthless. She had been scheduled for two personal appearances, and both had been canceled. There was a convention in Nashville in a few weeks, but he wasn't sure if she would attend. Inquiries to the event coordinators had gone unanswered. Besides, he didn't want to wait another month. He couldn't wait. He forced himself to go slowly and enjoyed the pursuit but only as long as his quarry was in view. Instead, she had slipped his grasp, and he had no idea where she had disappeared. The thought infuriated him.

He made his way up the stairs to his room and sat on the bed. Pulling out a box, he opened it and withdrew one of the books. Running his hands over the cover, he smiled. Yes, he could sacrifice one of them to be sent off for her signature. He could easily replace it tomorrow. Pressing it to his lips, he kissed it reverently before hugging it. Waiting an hour to return to Sam's little house wouldn't be too bad. His hands shook as he formulated a plan.

Precisely an hour later, he handed over one of his cherished books to Sam who chose a box and placed it on the table. Taking a piece of paper, he hastily penned a note explaining the novel's presence and placed it inside. As Sam opened the box to nestle it among cellophane bound bundles of pictures and printed materials, Artemis memorized the address printed on the shipping label.

Mississippi. She was in Mississippi.

He smiled and thanked Sam for his invaluable help. He would have her back where she belonged. It was almost harvest time. Little Rose would be in perfect bloom.

Chapter 19

It had been a long day, and Joselyn was ready to fall into bed. Maddox's father and three of his four sisters had arrived early on Sunday morning for an impromptu Father's Day visit, staying for three days. With a house full of people, the sleeping arrangements had been tight. Maddox surrendered his bed to his parents, claiming a spot in the hayloft of the barn. Hannah and Shaun retreated to their RV, taking the three older children with them who thought the idea of "camping with Uncle Shaun" was the most fun ever. River's two oldest sisters, Deena and Felicity shared Shaun's old room, and the youngest, Marla and her two-year-old daughter stayed with Joselyn. "I'll sleep on the sofa," she had stated. "The baby will be fine in her playpen next to me."

Joselyn had insisted on them staying with her and, though it was a little crowded, was happy to have them. As a result, the two became fast friends. So much so Joselyn was a little sad to see the whole gang load into their vehicles and leave on Wednesday afternoon.

Now, with everything quiet, Joselyn and Maddox were sitting on the old porch swing listening to the katydids and frogs sing as a thousand stars appeared in the indigo sea above. He had turned sideways with his back to the swing's arm, one leg stretched on the seat and the other on the porch floor. Joselyn was nuzzled back against his chest, and he had one arm folded around her middle. The other lay on the swing back. Every so often, he would lean down and kiss her head as if to reassure himself she was there.

"It was so nice to meet your family."

He chuckled. "They are a handful but yeah, not too bad. I'm sorry you didn't get to meet Allie, but her job keeps her busy all the time. You would think a large chain restaurant could get by without one manager for a few days."

"She did call, and we got to talk to her on the telephone," Joselyn said as she laid her head back on his shoulder. "I always wished I had sisters growing up. I do have one cousin, but we rarely see each other. He is several years older than I am and went to live with his father when his parents divorced. I think they are in New Jersey or somewhere in the Northeast." She shrugged. "I know it upsets my Aunt Laura because he won't come to visit her. I called him when she was first diagnosed. He wasn't interested, so Mom sold her house and moved in with her to help her out. Sometimes you get the golden side of a family like yours. Sometimes you get the bottom of the barrel, like mine."

"Does he have anyone there? Maybe he can't get away. I can't believe a son wouldn't want to be there to help his mother going through something as rough as cancer treatments."

"He never married. All he can think of is his career as an investment broker. I'll say this much though, he does pay for her health insurance, so I guess, in his mind, he's doing his best."

Maddox pushed the swing back and forth with his boot against the floor. Joselyn relaxed against him as the quiet squeak of the chains became a rhythm to lull her off into a half sleep.

"Maybe he can't stand to see her so ill."

Joselyn jumped. "What?"

"Your cousin. Maybe he can't stand to see his mother suffering. Some people aren't strong enough to deal with it. From what I understand, chemotherapy patients are sick, unable to eat, have to have help getting around, even taking care of personal issues. It's a lot to place on a loved one's shoulders. I believe if I had to see one of my parents or Aaron or Celia go through cancer..." He shook his head. "I don't think even I could handle it. I'd like to think I could, but I don't know for sure."

She lifted his hand and pressed her lips against the rough palm. "You're the strongest man I have ever met. I don't mean only physical strength but also mental and emotional. I think if the situation ever arose, you would be there every step of the way. It's a part of who you are, Maddox. You're a protector, a fighter, a man who gets the job done. I believe you would treat a sick loved one the same way. Assess the situation, map out a plan of attack and get it done."

He laughed softly and pulled her around until she sat sideways on his lap. Wrapping his arms around her waist, he snuggled against her. "Hmm, you got me all figured out, do you?"

"Completely," she agreed. "And I love everything about you."

"Ditto," he growled and hugged her tighter.

Suddenly, the dogs came out from under the porch and began barking. In the barn, they heard several of the horses whinnying and stamping. From the chicken coop, the rooster crowed several times, and the hens clucked nervously. Maddox stilled and slowly eased her off his lap.

"What is it?"

He stood and shook his head. "I don't know."

Aaron appeared at the door with Shaun right behind. "Something's got the livestock spooked," his uncle said and slid his feet into his boots by the door.

Maddox agreed. "Yeah, so I hear. Let me get my weapon." He had secured both his handgun and the two rifles he had brought with him in Aaron's large steel gun safe because of the children's presence. He jogged inside with Aaron to retrieve them. Returning a moment later, he handed a rifle to Shaun. "Joselyn, I need you to go into the house while we check it out. Lock the door and don't come out no matter what you hear."

With a little trepidation, she went into the house and closed the door. Locking it tightly, she joined Celia in the living room. The older woman was busy closing and locking the windows. Glancing over, Joselyn noticed Hannah asleep on the sofa. Taking the remote, Celia turned off the television and sat on the sofa beside her daughter-in-law. Careful not to wake her, she pulled the coverlet over her shoulders.

"Should we wake her?" Joselyn whispered.

Celia shook her head. "It's probably a coyote or

fox trying to get into the chicken pen. Hannah needs her sleep. She is still having morning sickness, and I'm sure sleeping in the camper didn't help her back any." She reached over and pushed a tendril of hair out of Hannah's face. "Poor dear. It takes a lot to bring a baby into the world. Come and sit, Joselyn. Aaron and the boys have done this dance before. They'll run off whatever is out there."

Joselyn obeyed, settling into one of the two recliners. In silence they waited, listening to the noise still coming from outside. Gradually, the melee quieted until the normal nightly serenade resumed. As one, both women relaxed, and Joselyn spoke.

"I don't think I thanked you enough for allowing me to come stay here while things get sorted out in New Orleans."

The smile lighting the older woman's face was genuine. "Of course you would come here. Maddox is family, and unless I missed something, you would be too. This family takes care of its own."

"Still, I'm extremely grateful." Joselyn glanced at the window before continuing. "It's what Maddox says about his team." She deepened her voice to mimic his baritone. "'SEALs don't leave SEALs behind. Once a SEAL, always a SEAL.'"

Celia chuckled as Joselyn continued.

"I think he looked at his SEAL team like another family. From the stories he can tell me, they are extremely close. I suppose depending on a group of others to keep you safe in intense situations will make them closer than brothers. He misses them a lot. I was thinking of having a get together after this is over. Maddox will like that."

Celia began reminiscing. "When Maddox first enlisted, we thought he would do one tour and get out. As a teenager, he always talked about wanting to become an engineer or a veterinarian so we were sure he would serve a few years and use his Montgomery Bill to get an education. Then he called and said he had made it through training to be a SEAL. Aaron was a Green Beret, so he understood exactly what it meant. When Aaron explained it to Sarah, she broke down and cried. She was both proud of Maddox and terrified he would get hurt. Sarah remembered Aaron going on missions and being out of touch for days or even weeks at a time. She knew it would be hard for the family, but she also knew it was deep in Maddox's heart. He loved his country, his home, and his family. He was going to take care of all of them by serving." Celia smiled softly as she continued. "He would call Sarah and tell her, 'Mom, time to go to work. I'll call you when I can,' and he would be gone. She prayed, fretted, and worried about him until he called her to let her know he was fine. I know each of those calls scared her to death, but she understood his need to do what he could. I often wondered if I could have been as strong as she if Shaun had entered the service. It takes a tough man to go out and make the safety of others his priority, but it also takes a strong woman to stand by and let him be that protector."

Joselyn nodded slowly. "I think I understand what you're talking about." She chewed her lip. "I have been thinking about a new book and wanted to make the hero ex-military. Can I use what you said about being a strong woman in my book?"

Celia's face turned a slight pink. "Lord gracious! You can use whatever you want."

There was a knock on the door, and Joselyn yelped, clutching her heart in fright.

"It's just us, Mom," Shaun called out.

Joselyn ran over and unlocked the door letting the three men back inside. Aaron and Shaun disappeared into the den to return the guns to the safe as Maddox gathered her in his arms. Dropping a kiss on her lips, he held her close.

"What was it?"

He shook his head. "Not sure. We looked through the barn and around the chicken coop. Nothing looks out of place, but it's extremely dark tonight. Uncle Aaron put out a couple of traps in case it was a weasel or fox after the hens. "

"I'm glad everything is all right," Joselyn said. "I think I'll call it a night. Would you walk me to my room?"

He reluctantly let her go but tangled his fingers with hers. "Of course." Together, they climbed the stairs and stopped at her door.

"Sleep well, sweetheart."

She smiled. "You too." Her smile faltered. "Tomorrow, may we talk about the conference again? I've already missed several personal appearances, and my book was recently released. It's not good to be out of the public's eye too long. Oh, and I have a package to send out tomorrow as well. Maybe we can go into town and talk on the way?"

Maddox raised an eyebrow. "A package?"

She nodded. "The box of swag sent to me had a book in it. Sam said it was a new fan who wanted an autograph. I need to send it back because he's going to be leaving town soon."

Maddox thought it over a bit. "I guess a quick ride into town won't hurt anything. Sure, we'll mail your package after lunch tomorrow. But Joselyn, I don't want you going to any public events. Not until Bull tells me they have Beecher in custody. I'm sorry, sweetheart but a few books aren't worth your life. He's already proven he can find you. This is the only place safe for you."

Ire rose in her as she stared daggers at him. "There won't be much of a life left if I become a recluse. There are thousands of authors out there, hungry and willing to do whatever it takes to obtain even a taste of the success I've had. If I don't stay fresh in my reader's minds, they will wander away. I can't stay here forever!"

Maddox's eyes hardened. "I'm not talking about forever, Joselyn. Can't you see how important it is to keep you safe? I can't even begin to imagine losing you. You're too important. Damn the books!"

She drew in an enraged breath. He stopped her coming tirade with a slash of his hand. "Those books mean nothing if it comes at the price of your safety. *You're* what matters to me. Not them. I'd rather you were a housewife, living right here on this farm than to risk even one hair being damaged. No, it's not going to happen. You're NOT going to the conference. End of discussion."

He turned to leave, and she grabbed his arm. When he got like this, it was as if he turned to stone and she couldn't move him. In frustration, she growled at him. "I'm not made of china. Damn it, Maddox. I need to get back to work."

"Okay, pull out your laptop and work on your next book. At least I don't have to worry your foolish, stubborn streak will kill you while you type your little words on a screen."

Joselyn gaped at him. His words were cold and harsh, and they made her seethe. "I can't believe you belittle what I do." She punched his arm. "Maybe my little words aren't important to you, but they mean a lot to many other people and me, as well. What I do may not be as important as counter-terrorism or hunting weapons of mass destruction. I may not go out there and tromp through jungles looking for guerrilla fighters or whatever it is you did on your missions, but my books are important to me. *To me*, Maddox. I'm good at what I do. I'm extremely good at it. Most writers never even get on the New York Times list. I've done it twice. Most writers can't call themselves a best-selling author. I can. I thought you understood me. I guess you don't after all."

The expression on his face would have been almost comical if she hadn't been so upset. With a shake of his head, he threw his hands into the air. "Jesus, Joselyn. That's not what I meant, and you know it. I think about how close he has come to you, and I lose my freaking mind. Everything I've done to keep you safe, he's discovered a way around. I thought you would be secure in Atlanta. He found a way to you. I was sure nobody could get into your house. He did at least four times. I brought you here because I need to know you're out of danger. I've learned my lesson about Beecher. Even here, I'm not letting down my guard, but I also know I have Aaron and Shaun at my back. If I had my ideal situation, it would be with my team watching my six. Unfortunately, it's not possible. Even here, I want to wrap you in cotton wool and tuck you away from the world where nobody can get to you. It doesn't mean I don't care what you do because what is important to you is important to me. I can't risk losing you over a few book sales. You're an awesome author, and I know you can recapture your audience's attention if you have to lay low for a while. So please, honey, I'm begging you. Please, don't take away the best thing to ever come into my life. If anything were to happen to you, I don't think I could survive it. Losing my team is nothing compared to what it would mean if you weren't in my life any longer."

Joselyn stared at him as his words washed over her. He had poured his heart out to her, expressing his concerns at keeping her safe. She understood what it meant to have this huge, powerful man admit his insecurities. She practically stormed toward him as her anger faded and passion erupted. He stood dead still, the expression on his face one of waiting for an explosion from her. She raised one hand toward his face, and he winced, bracing for whatever retaliation she felt was necessary. Their eyes clashed - warm caramel and ice blue, tangling and entwining until they were hopelessly entrapped in the other's gaze.

Suddenly she leaped, wrapping her arms around his neck, her long legs around his waist. He staggered back a step when she caught him by surprise but hastened to lock his arms around her. Lips upon lips, the kiss they shared was fire so hot it threatened to melt them where they stood. Joselyn released all the love and fear she felt as tongues clashed, dueling for supremacy. He devoured her, sucking her bottom lip into his mouth, nibbling it as he pulled gently. Twisting, he pressed her against the wall. She moaned as his huge hands moved over her sides, cupping her rear in his palms and squeezed. Hunger and need flared into being as she gave in to the passion causing her heart to thump wildly. "Maddox," she gasped as he rained heated kisses along her jaw and down her throat. "Please." She wasn't sure what she begged for only that he do something to quench the conflagration in her core before she combusted.

He growled and with one last squeeze of her rear, took a step back and let her slide down his front until her feet were again on the floor. She clung to him with shaking fingers, refusing to let go. This was her Maddox, the man who owned her heart. She wanted him so badly, and despite the way he quickly disentangled their limbs, she knew he wanted her as well.

"No," he whispered. Pushing his fingers through his hair, he took another step back. "I'm not about to do this, not here, not now. Your promise. My promise. Honey, please."

Hurt flared through her. She understood what he was saying. He wanted her, but he was not going to let their passion break the promises made. She understood, but it didn't mean she had to like it. At this moment, her body was screaming to climb Maddox like he was a tree and find out what it meant to be his truly. She took another step forward, but he stopped her. "Please, sweetheart. I'm trying to do what's right for us both." The pleading on his face tempered her lust, and she reluctantly took a step back until she was flush against her door again.

Moving quietly toward her, Maddox cupped her chin, his thumb tenderly stroking her bottom lip as he pressed his forehead to hers. Closing his eyes, he murmured, "You tempt me, woman. My God, how you tempt me." He gritted his teeth. "But when the time comes, it will be done right. Not out here, in my uncle's hallway like two teenagers at the prom. We need to get this crap with Beecher over and done because I don't know how much longer I can hold out." He groaned and swore under his breath. "I should be elevated to sainthood."

She couldn't help it. A little giggle escaped, and she regarded him. "Alright, Saint Maddox, I think I better go to bed."

He groaned again and adjusted himself. Her eyes were drawn to the movement, and they widened. "Oh, my."

"Not. Helping. Go to bed, Joselyn. Please for the sake of my sanity, go to bed now before I do something I'll probably regret."

She winked at him saucily and slipped into her room. Closing the door, she slid along the worn wood and sat with her back to it. On the other side of the panel, she heard him mumble, "Time for a cold shower, an ice cold shower," as he walked off toward his room at the end of the hall.

Chapter 20

*R*iver yawned as he nursed a cup of coffee while sitting at the old butcher block table in the kitchen. Stretching his long, denim-clad legs, he felt the joints in his hips crack and pop. Too many years of abuse on these old bones. The life of a SEAL wasn't easy on a body, and today he was feeling all thirty-eight years acutely.

"What a long night," Shaun muttered as he entered the kitchen and headed straight to the coffee pot.

"Tell me about it," River replied.

Shaun dropped into one of the chairs and sipped the strong black brew. "Where's Dad?"

River lifted his chin toward the back door. "Left about ten minutes ago. He wanted to check the hen house again before heading out for the south pasture. He's worried about the two new calves out there what with all the activity last night."

The grunt from Shaun sounded loud in the still air.

"What do you think it was?" Maddox took another swig of the brew.

Shaun's shoulders lifted in a shrug. "Weasel or coyote? Maybe a fox. Unless it sets off one of the traps, we may never know. You remember how things were when we were kids. We had some great times those summers. I still can't believe I'm back here after all this time. It's as familiar to me as riding a bike." Shaun laughed. "Four years of college and I still end up back on the farm. You know, I'm happy here. It's where I belong."

"That means you're planning on staying?"

"I don't know. Maybe? Hannah loves it here. Her family is in Kentucky and raise horses so she'll always be a farm girl at heart. The pregnancy has been rough on her, so she's taking time off until after the baby is born. My job can be done anywhere, so I'm not worried. This is as good a place as any, and with my parents getting up there in years, they will need someone to step in. What about you, Mad? What are your plans now?"

River rubbed the scruff on his chin. What *were* his plans? When he left the service, he had intended on coming here for a while and helping out until he got his civilian feet back again. Listening to Shaun talk about being home had resonated with him. It had been ridiculously easy to slip back into the swing of things. Being here felt right. It felt like home. He exhaled slowly. "First thing is to take care of Joselyn's stalker problem. Other than that..." He shrugged. "I didn't have much more planned, to be honest. Finding myself on this side of my career never seemed real to me. It was some hypothetical point in the future. It would come eventually. 'Eventually' was a hell of a lot faster than I'm ready for."

The two sat in silence as the pre-dawn light slowly brightened outside from a dim gray to a soft blue. Off in the distance, a rooster crowed in greeting the new day.

"Sounds like Weiner has survived the night," Shaun grunted. "I still can't believe Dad named that stupid rooster 'Weiner.'" He shook his head in disbelief. "I think he did it because Mom turns red every time he mentions his name."

They both chuckled. "Uncle Aaron always did have a sense of humor."

Shaun nodded. "Yeah, he does. But I'm worried about him. There's a strain on his face I'm not used to seeing. He doesn't smile and joke as much as he used to, or maybe he isn't as good at hiding it now we're older."

"From what I gather, he hasn't been the same since those two prize bulls died. Losing the breeding program and having to let all the hands go took a bit out of him." River sat straighter and leaned on the table. He ran his hands over the coffee cup slowly. "He had a lot of dreams riding on those two. With both you and I away and no help with the place, he went into survival mode." He waved a hand around the room. "It's become a shell of what it used to be."

"Well, Mom and Dad are both in their sixties. Dad has always been strong, and Mom's a force to be reckoned with. Still, there's only so much they can do. Working a farm is hard, as you know. I'm afraid it's going to be the death of him. My biggest fear while on the road was getting a call from Mom saying he's had a stroke or a heart attack out in one of the pastures. I'm starting fatherhood kind of late in life, but I want my kid to know his or her grandparents."

Their talk was cut short as a noise came from in the living room. After a moment, Joselyn appeared in the doorway followed by Celia. River smiled at the two and stood pulling Joselyn into his embrace before kissing her soundly. "Good morning, sweetheart."

Beside her, Celia grinned. "Woah, gracious me, Maddox. You're going to set the house on fire."

Joselyn's face turned the adorable shade of pink he so loved. Releasing her, he dropped a peck on his aunt's cheek. "I learned from the best," he teased. At the table, Shaun groaned.

Celia pulled out a pan and went to the refrigerator. Digging around, she pulled out several items. "Going to be pancakes today," she called out. "Breakfast will be done in a few minutes."

As River sat back down in his chair, he pulled Joselyn into his lap. Nuzzling against her neck, he murmured, "You smell good enough to eat."

She snuggled into his arms. "You been awake all night? I heard the animals going crazy off and on."

He slowly traced circles on her arm causing the fine hairs there to raise. "A good portion of it. Dogs wouldn't quit barking, and it had the livestock in an uproar. Every half hour or so they started up again. Pretty sure it was some predator out to get a little chicken dinner."

"It wasn't a predator."

River's head snapped around. He spied his uncle standing in the doorway leading into the mudroom. Dressed in faded work jeans, a chambray shirt, and filthy boots, he filled the entryway with his presence. His stance was ramrod straight, and River noticed the slight tremor in his limbs. Fury burned in his eyes as he swept the room and his jaw clenched. A double barrel shotgun sat cradled in his arms.

"Aaron! You're tracking dirt on my floors," Celia admonished.

He shot her an apologetic glance. "I'll sweep it in a bit. Sorry, Ce." He motioned toward the two men at the table. "Come on, boys. I need your help a bit."

The way he said it made chills run along River's spine. Nudging Joselyn out of his lap, he stood. Beside him, Shaun took one last drink of his coffee and placed the mug in the sink. "Let me get my boots," River said approaching the mudroom.

When he reached his uncle, Aaron placed a hand on his shoulder. "Grab your sidearm," he murmured and disappeared back outside.

"Well, crap," he muttered. He was *not* going to like this.

"Son of a..." River swore as he glared at the back side of the barn.

"Holy, shit," Shaun muttered beside him.

"I guess now we know why we couldn't find any foxes. It seems we had a bigger predator prowling around last night," Aaron said with a nod toward the barn.

"Shaun? Hannah is sick. She asked me to find..." Joselyn's words dropped away to nothing as she came around the corner of the barn. River tried to block her, but she pushed past him. Eyes widening, her face paled as she read the sadistic message left for her in what looked like dried blood. The carcasses of two chickens lay on the ground underneath.

Gardens will wither once they have bloomed
Three other blossoms also are doomed.
The majestic Magnolia so full of life
Working away as the farmer's wife.
The delicate Lily with a secret she hides
A sweet, tender Daisy is slumbering inside.
My Rose has fled away from her home
So others now soon will also be sown.

"No," Joselyn whispered.

Maddox saw her knees buckle and pulled her into his arms before setting her on an upended bucket. Pushing her head down until it was lower than her knees, he told her, "Breathe, honey."

Gulping air, she pushed his hand from her head angrily. "I'm fine. It just surprised me. How did he find us?"

River shook his head. "I don't know. I didn't think he would be able to. There's no connection to me here. Bull has my cell phone. Have you told anyone the address? Maybe your mother?"

She shook her head. "I gave her the phone number. I haven't had my cell phone on, and I haven't been online unless we were in town. Maddox, I haven't even turned my laptop on while here in case he could somehow track us. I swear to you I've been extremely careful." She read the words aloud again and wrapped her arms around her midsection. "When I was a teenager, the thought of getting poetic love notes from a boy was so romantic. In truth, the reality makes it a lot less appealing."

Seeing her distress, River wrapped his arms around her and kissed her gently. She took in a shuddering breath but smiled. His breath hitched when it didn't reach her eyes. Letting her go, he stood and turned back toward the others.

"Now what?" Shaun asked.

"Family takes care of family," Aaron growled. "We hole up here and wait for this psycho to come back. With the three of us, we can handle him."

"No," Joselyn whispered.

"It's not going to be easy. We'll have to take turns watching, twenty-four seven," Shaun said. "You two are better at this stuff than I am, so you tell me what you need me to do."

"No," Joselyn shook her head.

"This place is too open. There are too many entrances, too many ways he can sneak by." River gestured toward the wall. "He managed to do this last night with us running around every few minutes."

"No," Joselyn said a bit louder. They ignored her.

"It was different. We thought it was a fox after the hens. Now we know..." Aaron started.

Joselyn stood, knocking the bucket over. "No!" she shouted.

All three of them stared at her like she had sprouted another head. It would be comical if not for the seriousness of the situation.

"I'm not going to put you at risk. I'm not going to let Celia, Hannah, or that precious little one get hurt because of my problem." She pushed by River and stomped toward the house.

"Where are you going?" River called out as he hurried after her. He caught her on the porch and swung her around to face him. Seeing the tears swimming in her eyes, he softened and brushed her cheek with his thumb. "Hey. Come on honey, don't let him win."

She pushed out of his arms. "He's already won. Can't you see? He won the minute he threatened your family. When he mentioned Hannah and the baby, he won."

"Joselyn, he hasn't won. You're still alive. Aunt Celia, Hannah, and the baby are fine. "

"But for how long? He's already proven he can find me. He can get to me no matter where I go. You saw the message. He'll hurt them if I keep running."

He brushed the hair from her face and cupped her cheek in his rough palm. "We stop running. We take a stand... here and now."

She shook her head. "Not here and not now." Turning away, she climbed the steps. "I'm not going to let anyone else get hurt. Since he is going to get to me anyway, I'm going home. We'll change the locks, reset the codes and if we have to, we will hire a full security team. I'm not going to stay here and let him target the others. It's time I got back to New Orleans."

Chapter 21

*L*ord, it was good to be home.

Even as distressed as Joselyn was at the thought of returning here, there was something almost cathartic about being back "on her own turf" as it were. She sat in the cab of the truck while Detective Jameson and two uniformed officers swept through her house to ensure everything was in order. Once it was cleared and Detective Jameson gave the okay, Maddox patted her hand and slipped out his door. Going around to her side, he opened it and helped her out. She steeled herself before climbing the steps into her home.

"First things first," Maddox muttered after closing the door. Stopping at the alarm panel, he punched several buttons. "I'm changing the code."

She watched him put in the numbers and put them in a second time to confirm his choice. She looked at him as understanding dawned. "Will it work?"

Maddox grinned at her. "Mmmhm. With this system, putting in the code backward will activate the silent panic mode. So I made the new code the old one backward. Ingenious, am I not?"

She raised up on her tiptoes. "Devious man," she murmured and kissed his cheek. Pulling out her cell phone, she swiped several buttons. His large hand landed on top of her screen. Looking up, she saw an unreadable expression on his face.

"Are you doing what I think you're doing?" he asked.

"If you think I'm updating my password file on my cell, then yes, I'm doing what you think I am."

He groaned. "Updating? Wait, did you have the access code on your old cell?"

She nodded in confusion"Yes, I told you I have everything on my phone. It's one of the reason's I was so upset to lose the old one. Why?"

"Honey, he stole your cell phone. Beecher had your cell phone, remember?"

Realization dawned on her. "I gave him my alarm code. That's how he knew it. Oh, my God, that phone had all my banking information, credit cards, contacts... everything! I'm so stupid! It's how he found me in Atlanta and how he knew I would be at the after party. It was on my schedule. I didn't think about it."

He sighed. "I didn't either. I guess I thought you had tighter security on it. Was is locked?"

She shrugged. "I don't know. I got tired of it shutting off on me, so I disabled the timer. I always tried to lock it manually, but I don't know if it was locked that night or not."

"Okay," he grabbed the back of his neck with one hand and propped the other on his hip. Pacing back and forth, he seemed to be mulling things over. "How can we profit from this? He thinks he has all this information. There's got to be a way to use this to our advantage. Maybe lay a trap?"

There was a knock on the door. "River? It's Bull."

Maddox opened the door for his friend and closed it as soon as Detective Jameson came through. Quickly, they went over what they had discovered. When they were done, Detective Jameson shook his head. "At least now you know and can keep him from using that information to get to her. Unless this guy is stupid, I doubt he would fall into a trap. So far, he's been too smart. In other news, we finished the sweep of the grounds, and it all looks good. I think we need to have a long talk about everything you've encountered since you left my office. Don't leave a single thing out, no matter how seemingly insignificant. It's time we beat this guy at his own game and to do it; we have to figure out how he found you. You never had River's family's address in your cell so he couldn't get it from there. There is a hole somewhere, and we need to plug it."

She agreed. "Let's go into the living room. This may take a while."

"A while" translated into almost two full hours. The first forty-five minutes were spent on the telephone to her various banking and credit card companies. After ensuring there were no fraudulent charges, she went ahead and canceled her existing cards and ordered new ones, just to be on the safe side. The rest of the time was exhausted going over every action and movement she had made.

"I know this is a sore point with you, but I think you should cancel the upcoming convention," Maddox suggested.

"No, I want to hold onto the reservation in case

this is all resolved by then. I'll eat the cancellation fees if it's too dangerous. The convention being so close, it won't make much difference anyway." She was scrolling through her telephone, checking her other engagements. "Nashville was the next big thing on my calendar. I didn't schedule anything after for a couple of months other than a few local appearances. I'm hoping to start to work on my next novel." She hesitated. "Maybe we can use the convention to flush him out?"

"Maybe," Detective Jameson agreed. "But it would be better to get this resolved sooner than later."

Maddox agreed.

She placed the cell phone on the table and sat back. "Well, that's it. He's been cut off now. I haven't scheduled anything since I got my new cell. He won't know anything else."

"He shouldn't anyway," Detective Jameson said. "When the old one was deactivated, he lost the window of opportunity. I suspect he downloaded everything off of it because he hasn't turned it back on. I talked to my friend yesterday, and he says there hasn't been a single blip. This guy's tricky and smart. "

"Too smart." Joselyn agreed. "What I can't figure out is how he found me at the farm."

"The farm has me puzzled too. He couldn't have gotten the address from your cell phone as far as I can tell. He doesn't know anything about me. He doesn't even know I'm ex-SEAL. He calls me 'the soldier,'" Maddox's lip curled in derision. "I'm not a ground pounder. He needs to learn the difference between the Army and the Navy."

"Alright, let's think about this for a minute. You didn't give the address to anyone, what-so-ever?" Detective Jameson asked.

Maddox and Joselyn shook their heads. "Oh, well nobody except for Sam," she said. "He sent me a box of swag I needed to approve before it could go into production. I had him overnight it."

"Who is Sam?" Detective Jameson asked. "Do you trust him?"

"Sam is one of the gate guards for the community." Maddox supplied constructively. "Two twelve hour shifts split by four men. You vetted them for me the first week I was here. There's also Felix, Trevor and..."

"Manny," Joselyn finished.

"Four men who had access to your whereabouts," Detective Jameson said. "I'll have them brought in for questioning."

"What about this," Joselyn motioned toward the photo of the message left on the barn.

"I've been in contact with the Sheriff's department in Lauderdale County. They are going to keep an eye on things there. Personally, I believe this shows his frustration." Detective Jameson took the picture out of her hand. "This is the act of a desperate man. His little game has gone on too long. When you slipped out of his grasp, he began losing his hold on things. You took the control away." He placed the photo on top of a file folder sitting on the table. "Now you're back; I don't think he's going to wait much longer.

One way or another, this thing is about to be concluded."

Chills coursed up Joselyn's spine at the frank words from the police detective. Drawing a breath she nodded. "Alright," she said resolutely. "What are we going to do?"

Maddox looked at Detective Jameson. Something passed between them, and Detective Jameson nodded. With a quick lift of his chin, Maddox turned to her. In a cold, hard voice, he said, "Finish this."

Chapter 22

*J*uly arrived in New Orleans with all of the lumbering grace of a pregnant elephant. The weather morphed from simply muggy to hot and almost unbearable. The evening showers typical for this time of year did nothing to cool off the thick air. Instead, it merely created an atmosphere so congested it was like trying to breathe underwater.

The overwhelming humidity, along with the unnatural lull from her stalker seemed to suck the life right out of Joselyn and it worried River. She retained the habits she acquired while on the farm and continued to rise early each morning before disappearing into her office for the day. Not even the lure of dinner from Giovanni's could pull her out. "I'll eat when I'm hungry," she would tell him as she stared at her mostly blank screen. The apathy concerned him most. Each time he came in to check on her, she hadn't moved, and the words on the screen hadn't grown substantially. It almost ripped his heart out to see her sinking into hopelessness.

Just over two weeks after returning from Mississippi, he'd had enough. Bursting into her office, he sauntered over to her desk and sat in the antique wingback next to it. He placed a heavy plastic bag on the ground at his feet. She looked at him with wide, unblinking eyes as he pulled his firearm out, unchambered the round, removed the magazine, checked the breach and placed the two pieces on the desktop beside her keyboard. "This is the SIG Sauer P226 Mk25, the weapon of choice of the US SEALs," he said. "The barrel is made from a metal alloy and attached to full size, stainless steel frame. Almost eight inches long, one and a half inch wide and five and a half inches high, it weighs in at right under two pounds total weight. It is both double and single action. The double action trigger pull is ten pounds and only four point four with the single. The magazine holds twenty rounds of 9mm, 124-grain v-crown." He retrieved both parts, slapped the magazine back into the handle and racked the slide. "It's sleek, precise and deadly."

"I don't understand." She said, eying him as he worked the piece.

He ensured the safety was engaged and slid it back home into the holster at his hip. Picking up the bag, he removed a box and placed it on the desk. Opening it, he pulled out a handgun resembling his but much smaller. "This is the SIG Sauer P938 Edge. It holds six 9mm Luger rounds in the mag and one in the pipe. Made of a metal alloy on a sub-compact stainless steel frame, it weighs in at only one pound. It takes seven pounds of pressure to fire. Single action trigger only but it's all you'll need." He ejected the magazine, pulled the slide and held it up to the light. "Lightweight, compact and the perfect self-defense sidearm."

She shook her head at him. "I don't need a gun. Security is your thing. It's why I have you."

River placed the weapon back into its foam cradle.

Taking her hands in his, he waited until her eyes left the box and focused on him. "This is not a gun; it's a weapon, a firearm, a sidearm or a pistol. Guns are mounted on ships and weigh several tons. However, back to your comment. Yes, you do need it. I've been watching you for the past few days, and frankly, it's worrying me. Honey, you're going through the motions of living right now. Waking every morning, coming in here and staring at the screen isn't doing you any good. I see you withering away, and it's gutting me. I can tell you feel hopeless and you're giving in. This is not you; you're a fighter. You're stronger than this; stronger than all the Donavan Beechers in the world. Yes, I'm here to protect you but what if the unthinkable happens? What if I get hurt or killed? You need to have the skills to take care of yourself until the police arrive." He hated the look of alarm and pain his words caused her. She didn't like thinking he was not impervious to harm. "I know you don't want to consider it, but there is a possibility."

She shook her head.

"Yes, it is. I'm only human." Seeing she wasn't about to give in, he changed tactics. "Alright, how about this? What if someone breaks in and when I go to check on things, I stumble over a rug, fall down the stairs, smack my noggin on the wall and get knocked out? Who's going to protect *me*?" He raised his eyebrows at her.

She let out a heavy sigh. "You're the most coordinated, graceful man I have ever seen. I bet you haven't tripped since you were in diapers but I see what you're getting at," she capitulated with a slight nod.

Knowing he had her at least partially won over, River hurried on so she couldn't back-peddle. "Now, go do whatever it is you think you have to do to go out because I'm taking you to get some lunch and on to the firing range. I want to teach you how to load, unload, clear jams and use this weapon safely and correctly."

Joselyn looked at the box and back to him. Slowly, some of the strain dissolved from her face. "Okay. I think maybe it would be a good idea. I hate feeling helpless."

"That's my girl," he beamed. Standing, he picked up the box. "It'll also do you a lot of good to destroy some targets. It's the perfect way to relieve the stress you're shouldering. So I'll see you in the living room when you're ready."

She stood and pushed her chair back. "Maddox?"

He stopped in the doorway and looked back at her. "Yeah?"

A mischievous grin lit her face. "Can I get a hot pink holster?"

He raised one eyebrow. "Hot pink? You want to put a SIG Sauer firearm, the chosen weapon of the United States Navy SEALs, into a hot pink holster?" He sighed dramatically. "Dear, sweet, baby Jesus, woman."

"With sparkles!" She added and giggled at his look of abject horror.

Giving her a wave toward the stairs, he said, "Go

on before my team shows up and confiscates both my man card and my trident pin for even considering it."

She hurried by him, stopping only to rise on her tiptoes and kissing him quickly. "Thank you," she whispered and hurried up the steps.

Curling his fingers around the edge of the box, he watched her climb, his eyes as always on the seductive sway of her rear. Shaking his head, he turned toward the living room. If it got her out of the gloom she had been in, he would find her the most sparkly, brightest, neon pink holster he could.

Maddox took the time to show her proper handling procedures with the new firearm she had nicknamed 'Betty.' He shook his head at her but smiled when she hummed the song, "Black Betty," under her breath while she loaded and unloaded the magazine several times.

Now she was standing in one of the little cubbies wearing eye and ear protection and holding Betty firmly in her hand. Maddox's heat warmed her back as he curled his arms around her, bracing her arms and firming her grasp. One side of the ugly orange earmuffs was moved slightly so she could hear his instructions.

"Keep both eyes open, sight down the barrel." His whispers brought forth gooseflesh on her arms. Shifting slightly, she heard his sudden intake when her rear brushed against his thigh. "Minx," he muttered but continued the lesson. "Remember to breathe like I taught you and squeeze the trigger, don't pull it.

There will be a bit of recoil so be prepared for it. You ready to try?"

She nodded, and he took a step back after adjusting her ear covering. She missed his strength immediately but focused her attention on the hanging paper target at the end of the room. Sticking her tongue out slightly, she sighted along the barrel and squeezed.

The sound of the discharge was loud even with noise suppression on. Adjusting her stance slightly, she braced and fired again. Glancing over her shoulder, she grinned to see his approving smile. Turning her attention back, she fired off three more times before placing the weapon on the table in front of her. Holding her hands in the air to show she was unarmed like he had taught her, she took a step back. Pulling the earphones to rest around her neck, she grinned.

Stepping into her space, Maddox pushed the button to bring the target to them. She jumped with a squeal when she saw all six shots had hit the paper. Only two of them went into the body outline - one in the top right shoulder and the other on the left ear. Neither of them would be fatal. However, she was still excited about actually hitting something and was not upset. Maddox took the paper and studied it.

"You're holding your breath before you fire, Joselyn. Remember to breathe through the shots. These two," he pointed out two holes on the top furthermost from the outline, "are from pulling the trigger instead of squeezing. But to hit the target at all your first time isn't bad. Let's put another one out.

Reload and try again, yeah?"

"Okay," she agreed.

By the time she worked her way through the box of ammunition, she was consistently pegging the outline, and her groupings were much improved. One of the holes could even be considered fatal. She shook her hand to work some of the soreness from her wrist while Maddox pulled the last target.

"Much better, honey," he said encouragingly. "A few more trips here and I'll have you shooting like a pro."

Just like that, all the worry and anxiety she had been feeling over the past couple of weeks evaporated like mist. He was so smart and caring. Best of all, he was giving her tools to ensure she didn't feel helpless any longer. The chances were she would never have to use this new skill set, but at least she knew if things came down to it, she could. Though she hated to admit it, Maddox had been right; something was healing about tearing holes through paper cutouts on the firing range.

When he moved out of the cubby, she retrieved Betty and carefully checked to make sure she was empty. Pulling the magazine out, she placed it and the handgun into the box along with the bright pink camouflage holster she had purchased from the range's gift shop. The look on his face when she had chosen the gaudy thing was priceless.

Tapping her earphones, he winked at her and pulled his own snugly on his ears. Understanding filled her as she hastened to protect her hearing. She stood back and to the side of him. Once she was ready, he took a step forward, drew his firearm, aimed and let go with a half dozen shots in rapid succession. Joselyn's eyes widened as she watched her man in action. She giggled to herself. He was hot when he went all alpha badass.

Flicking the safety on, he replaced the SIG into his holster and pushed the button. Joselyn gasped when she saw the target. There were six perfect little holes all less than a quarter inch apart right in the middle of the target's head. Holy cow!

She must have said it out loud because he laughed. "Lots of training and a ton of practice rounds. We spent hours honing our skills."

"You were a sniper, weren't you?"

He dropped his chin in a nod.

"Can you show me?"

He hesitated a moment and nodded again. Taking a marker from the table, he drew four quarter size circles in the white surrounding the black outline. Hanging the target, he let it go as far as it could until it was almost against the far wall. Once it stopped swaying, Maddox stepped forward, donned his protection and looked down the range. Suddenly, in a blur of movement, he drew his weapon, flicked the safety and fired four rounds. Securing it once again, he stabbed at the button and stepped out of the way. Pulling the target from its clips, Joselyn stared in shock at the four circles. Each one was neatly pierced by a single hole with only one circle missing the tiniest bit of one side.

Taking the paper from her hands, he wadded it and tossed it into the trash. "Come on, let's go," he said to her and led her out the door. Stepping back into the much quieter shop, Maddox stopped to purchase another box of ammunition and a cleaning kit. "You need to learn how to take care of Betty, too," he said. "Always clean and oil her after shooting a box. If you don't take care of her, she won't be ready to take care of you."

Joselyn nodded absently as she followed him out the shop and to his truck. Buckling in, she watched him as he began the drive back home. She knew deep in her heart that Maddox would be good with a firearm. He wasn't merely good, he was deadly, and she was glad all that ability was aimed at protecting her body and soul. She glanced over at him and slid her hand over until it touched his leg. He turned his attention to her briefly with a smile before returning it to the road.

Her big, SEAL protector was more than capable of taking care of her, and she was so grateful for Detective Jameson putting him into her life. Maybe the police would catch Beecher before Maddox ever had to use any of his training for her. Regardless, she was glad to know he was there for her anyway and it made her feel special and cherished. She knew, without a shadow of a doubt, he would willingly give his life for her. It was ingrained into his very DNA to be this protective. It didn't surprise her at all when she considered the depth of commitment toward her because she felt the same way. They were one cohesive unit now. Yin and Yang, two halves of the same coin. She squeezed his leg and pulled her hand back. His hand shot out his hand and grabbed it.

"I like it there," he commented and placed it back on his thigh.

She sighed softly and laid her head against the headrest, not taking her gaze from his handsome face. "And I like you here," she murmured. "I know you'll keep me safe."

"Forever."

Maddox's cell rang, and he punched a button on the steering wheel to activate the bluetooth hands-free feature. "Yeah," he said into the air.

"River, where are you?" Detective Jameson' voice sounded strange. "You have Joselyn with you?" There was a lot of noise in the background like people talking and weird electronic dings. Then a door closed and the noise ceased.

"Yeah, we're on our way home. I'm about two miles out. Why?

Bull ignored his question. "Joselyn, can you hear me?"

"Yes, Detective Jameson." She looked at Maddox with a quizzical glance. What was going on?

The relief was clear in his voice. "Good, good. Do you know the Progues? They live across the street and down a couple of houses from you."

"Velma and Arlan? Yes. Well, no more than neighbors." An ugly feeling twisted in her gut. Why would Detective Jameson be asking her about them?

"River, pull off the road. I don't want you

wrecking."

Crap. This couldn't be good.

Apparently, Maddox thought the same, for when he pulled the truck over into an empty lot, he cursed. Throwing the truck in park, he said, "What's going on?"

The sound of a drawn breath emitted from the speakers. "There's no easy way to put this, so I'm going to throw it out there. Velma and Arlan Progue were found this afternoon by their daughter. She had gotten worried when she hadn't heard from them since they came home from a trip. They were attacked."

Joselyn gasped. "Attacked?" She felt the blood drain from her face. "Are they alright?"

"Yeah. They are alive, locked in the basement. Luckily, there is a bathroom there so they could get water but neither had eaten in several days; the little bit of food they had ran out quickly. Velma's had a slight stroke. The doctor thinks it's stress related, but they won't let anyone see her until she stabilizes. I talked to Arlan, and he told me they had hired a man to house sit for them while they were away on a cruise in Europe. The man's name is Artemis King."

Joselyn nodded to herself. "I knew they were out of town and had a sitter. I think I may have seen him a few times but never close. He's an older man, in his fifties with gray hair and a dark complexion with a beard I think?"

"Yeah, it's the same description we got. According to Progue, they came home and found him asleep. He was on the floor of his room." He hesitated a minute. "River, don't lose your cool."

Maddox's eyes had a hard gleam, and his jaw clenched. "Say it," he ground out.

Detective Jameson spewed the words out so fast, Joselyn could barely understand. "King was naked in a pile of photographs of Joselyn."

Joselyn was shocked. She didn't even react to the string of profanity spewing from Maddox's lips. He hit the steering wheel several times with his fist and threw his head back on the headrest. "The bastard was right there inside the gate the whole time! Right there!" He thrust his fingers through his hair. "Please tell me you got him?"

"No, he was long gone; probably left the night they returned home. Progue said they woke him and tried to throw him out of the house. Instead, he pulled a knife on them and forced them to the basement. Forensics went over there and checked the house, but it was cleaned. We did catch a break and lifted a partial right index from a door facing. We were able to get a match."

"Let me guess. Donavan freaking Beecher."

There was an ominous pause, and Bull swore softly. "No, it's not Beecher." He hesitated a minute and continued. "Joselyn was right all along. Her stalker is Douglas McClane."

Chapter 23

*H*ow was it even possible?

River paced back and forth in the living room, trying to wrap his brain around the improbable reality of Bull's information bomb this afternoon. By the time the police had cleared the area, leaving the Progue's house draped in yellow crime scene tape, the identity of their house sitter and his connection to Joselyn had made its rounds through the neighborhood. Several of her neighbors had come over, hoping for some juicy gossip and asking a thousand questions. Sam was heartbroken and apologized profusely for his 'assistance' in helping McClane find her in Mississippi. True to Joselyn's nature, she forgave him instantly. McClane was a master at manipulation, and she couldn't blame Sam for falling for his lies. River, on the other hand, was not so generous. Intentional or not, Sam's actions had put Joselyn and River's family in jeopardy. It had taken all of his resolve not to throttle the man where he stood.

He thought about the still photograph captured from the Progue's security cameras Bull had shown them. The picture held almost no resemblance to the man featured in the pictures during his trial. His frame was much bulkier now with the addition of lots of lean muscle. His normally pale complexion had turned a dark tan. Colored contacts changed his hazel eyes to vivid green, and the mustache and goatee made his face look longer. River stopped his pacing, placed his hands on the door and leaned forward until his head rested between his hands. Slowly he hit his forehead on the door but not enough to hurt. The last thing he needed was to knock himself out and leave Joselyn vulnerable. A pair of arms circled his waist, and a warm presence pressed against his back. Placing his large hand on her smaller one, he squeezed it reassuringly.

"There wasn't anything you could do," she said against his back.

"I was so focused on making sure he wasn't getting in; it never occurred to me he already was. This kind of Charlie Foxtrot is what gets people killed."

She shook her head against his back. "This isn't a SEAL mission, Maddox. This isn't a team of six men working together to watch each other's backs. This is one man, one single person taxed with keeping both of us safe. You couldn't have known. My Lord, I waved at the man a half a dozen times and never even knew who he was. I sat there in the courtroom, and I stared at his face every day for three and a half weeks. At least you hadn't seen him before, so you have an excuse. I don't. If anyone is to blame here, it's me."

He whirled around and wrapped his arms around her. "You aren't to blame, honey. Everyone insisted McClane was dead, but you didn't believe it. For weeks, you were adamant the man stalking you was McClane. You didn't change your mind about it until the possibility of Beecher was thrust in your face." He cupped her cheek and pressed his lips to her forehead. "You're innocent here."

She started to argue, but he stopped her with a chaste kiss on her lips. "I'm going to do a sweep of the grounds." He released her. "It's been a long day. I know it's getting late, but Giovanni's is still open. How about we call in an order and afterward I'll show you how to clean Betty? Don't think I've forgotten about her."

The laugh erupting from her lips lifted his heart. "Alright, Mr. Bodyguard. I'm going to answer some emails after I call in our order. The usual?"

"Yeah, sounds good," he said as she stepped out of his arms and turned.

With a smack on her tush, he growled at her. "Temptress."

She stopped, glanced over her shoulder and wiggled her butt. The growl became louder. "I'm a saint, I'm a saint," he whispered and winked at her.

She laughed aloud and disappeared through the office door.

Since he knew McClane could get in at any time, he made sure to arm the alarm even when he did perimeter sweeps. He didn't want to take any chances. Closing the front door, he heard the arming chirp and turned toward the right. Stepping off the porch, he made his way toward the pergola, and its vine-covered depths. Stopping outside the structure, he frowned. The motion sensors should have detected his movements and flooded the little corner with light. Taking a step back he waved his arms and stepped forward again. Still no lights.

The hair on the back of his neck stood up and a knot formed in the bottom of his stomach. Something wasn't right. Drawing his firearm, finger on the safety, he worked his way around the structure until his back was flushed against the high wall surrounding her property. Making his way silently along the wall, he carefully peered into the inky blackness engulfing this corner of the yard. Raising his pistol, he waited for a movement.

When it came, the attack wasn't from the front or back. Instead, something whipped over his head and around his neck. Years of training kicked in as River's hand went up to work his fingers between the rapidly closing cord and his neck. The other hand, the one still grasping his firearm, raised to shoot the dark shadow crouched low on the wall. A kick sent his SIG flying into the pergola, so he grabbed the man pulling the rope in an attempt to strangle him.

Lights danced around River's peripheral vision as oxygen was cut off. Gasping, River's reaching fingers fought for the rope in his assailant's hand. He knew if he didn't get control soon, he wouldn't have enough strength to get out of this. He grunted as something hard slammed into the side of his head. The sparkling lights brightened and began to dim. Bracing his feet on the wall, he shoved hard in an attempt to pull McClane from the top. The rope tightened more until he was afraid his fingers would be severed. The second kick to his temple was harder than the first. Between the blows and his rapidly diminishing air, River knew he wasn't going to make it. The last thing crossing his mind was the knowledge he had once again failed Joselyn. It pissed him off. She was going to die tonight, and there was nothing he could do to stop it.

Dinner ordered, Joselyn worked her way through the hundreds of spam messages in her email box. Mumbling to herself, she clicked on several at a time and the delete button. "I don't need pharmaceuticals, my mortgage rate is fine, and there's no way I'm helping some random guy get his lottery winnings." She snorted. "As if."

The remaining messages were easily sorted into one of several folders. She insisted on being organized and neat, so she made it a habit of sorting them before she started to read. This way, nothing got lost. Starting with the first folder labeled "FANS," she opened the top one and started to read.

After a few minutes in, she heard the door close and the chirp of the alarm. "Hey Maddox, come here. I want you to see this drawing from one of my fans. She's only sixteen and did a great job," she called out over her shoulder. "It's exactly how what I envisioned John and Deidre to look."

She heard him enter the room and scooted back so he could look at her screen. The color drained from her face, and she froze at the sight of the hooded figure watching her from the doorway. Leaning against the facing with one foot crossed casually over the other, stood a man dressed in black pants and matching long sleeve shirt. A pair of dark boots with something wet and shiny on one heel covered his feet. Reaching for his head, he pushed a ski mask off his face, revealing a maniacal smile. He casually shoved the mask into his pocket. Lifting his leather gloved hand, he saluted her with two fingers.

"Hello, Little Rose."

She screamed.

Chapter 24

*D*ouglas McClane sat on the edge of her bed, his legs crossed in a pose of utter relaxation. Flicking the blade in his fingers, he watched her as she balked at his command to don the purple dress from the trial. Instead, her gaze jumped between the clock by her bed and the doorway.

"I know what you're thinking. You believe your soldier will arrive, to rescue the princess from the evil clutches of the villain. I'm sorry to have to inform you. That isn't this story. I often told my students fairy tales are useless. They teach us nothing but lies and false hopes, though the original Grimm is a bit more realistic. Modern society has sweetened the stories and removed their bite, but I digress." He stood and stalked toward her, taking her arm and leading her to the window. Pushing the curtain aside, he grabbed her chin and pointed her face toward the corner garden. "I never thought I would appreciate climbing ivy in my garden, but he makes an elegant augmentation, don't you think?"

The corner was dark, thanks to his quick work with the floodlights but one could still make out the dark shadow hanging limply from the iron wall cap and to the left of the pergola. He could tell the moment Joselyn understood what she was viewing. Her eyes grew wide, and her lips parted. "Maddox!" she screamed and pushed against him. In a quick action, he brought the knife to her neck. Grabbing a fist full of her hair, he yanked her back from the window. As she stilled, he snarled, "Don't try it again. You keep quiet, obey me, and I'll stop my garden with you. Give me any more trouble; I'll be including a Magnolia, a Lily and a sweet, tender Daisy."

She stilled instantly, and he let her go. Motioning toward the purple draped chair, he barked at her, "Dress," and resumed his post at the foot of her bed.

His eyes feasted on the nubile form of his prey as she tugged the garment over her head. It was almost a shame to cover the magnificent body he had stripped earlier, but there were rules to every game. First, she must be dressed properly. There would be enough time for undressing later.

As her face emerged from the sweetheart collar, his breath hitched when he saw the dewy trails spilling across her pale cheeks. He watched in fascination as her pink lips trembled with each frantic breath. He closed his eyes with a moan. Her terror was better than the most succulent of meals. It fed his soul until he was almost giddy and drunk on it. Of all the fragile blossoms in his garden, his beautiful, delicate rose was the most exquisite of them all. He couldn't tear his eyes away from the way her breasts lifted as she pulled the back upward slightly to reach the zipper and tug it closed. He licked his lips in anticipation of feasting on those globes flavored with salty tears and the coppery tang of blood.

With the dress in place, he made a circle with his finger, indicating she should turn so he could take in every inch of the vision which had haunted him for years. With her revolution completed, he frowned and shook his head. "Your hair isn't proper. Put it up with the purple barrette, the one in your second drawer on the right side."

She did as he bade her, piling her blonde tresses on top of her head and securing them with the clip. Once it was done, he beckoned her over. She shook her head and took a step back.

Snarling, McClane leaped to his feet. "Obey me, Little Rose or the reaping will be excruciatingly painful. Don't forget there are other blossoms at stake here." The whimper escaping her lips was music to his soul. Crooking his finger again, he said, "Come here."

Slowly she made her way over until she stood in front of him. Reaching over, he touched her cheek, causing her to flinch and shut her eyes tightly. He frowned again. "Perhaps I was wrong. In this attire you favor the shrinking violet instead of a rose," he whispered. He shook his head to clear such foolishness from his mind. "No, karma has spoken. You're the rose, the magnificent apex of my work." Taking her hand in his, he pulled her back to the bed and again sat. Pointing to the floor between his feet, he commanded her. "Sit."

Doing as McClane said, Joselyn dropped to her knees and closed her eyes. He watched as she took a breath and held it. So stunning but not quite correct. He nudged her knees to the side. "Be graceful, elegant. Lounge artfully." He watched her hungrily as she dropped to sit on her left hip, her feet curled beside her right side. "Yes, much better. Hands, folded in your lap. That's it. Perfection."

He sat back, his eyes taking in the lovely sight resting before him. With a nod, he cocked his head to the side. "I have touched the Morning Glory, felt the silken petals of the Dahlia. The fire of the Zinnia and the sweet soft blush of the Camellia were mine to sample. Even the exotic Lotus and the mighty Acacia have entertained my gaze, but none have come close to the exquisite excellence of you, my beautiful Rose." He reached forward and caressed her cheek. She whimpered again and drew back. Anger flared in him. "This is your last warning. Draw away again, and others will suffer the consequences." He grabbed her neck in his hand and pulled her forward until he could feel the fan of her breath on his face. "Do you hear my words, Little Rose?"

Hastily, she nodded.

McClane let her go with a smile. "Since we are discussing fables, and you're an author, I'll tell you a special story. I'll call this, 'The Viewing.' When first I saw you sitting there in the jury box on the inaugural day of my trial, I felt such urges well in my soul, urges I thought had withered away like leaves when kissed by winter. With a single glance, I was enraptured. Once again, I craved to tend my garden. As each day waxed and waned, I watched you, so regal and strong, absorbing everything around you." He paused as he eyes raked over her again. "I admit it took me a while to understand you. I thought at first you were the Sunflower, tall and strong, basking in the glory of Apollo's countenance. But several days later something was said - I forget exactly what but your face bloomed into the most breathtaking smile, and I glimpsed the rose hidden beneath." He sat back and regarded her. "I had six perfect blossoms in my garden and was searching for the seventh. Imagine my joy in discovering you there, sitting so primly in the seventh seat of the jury box. It was kismet. My seventh flower in the seventh chair."

McClane stood and walked over behind her. Crouching, he ran a finger over her bare neck. "Seven is a special number for my family and me. Mother's name was Beverly and her twin, my Aunt Breanna. Mother married Gilbert McClane, and Breanna chose Terrell Beecher. Do you see the sevens? Each name contains exactly seven letters." He leaned in closer. "Douglas is seven, my brother, Donavan is seven. Your name, Joselyn Kendrik, is another pair of sevens. I confess for a moment, I entertained the thought of wooing you instead of reaping, but you chose another." Anger forced his words to sound harsh even to his ears. "You let a filthy soldier defile that which is mine. It makes me angry to think of him touching you."

Her eyes widen, and she wisely chose to change the subject of her infidelity. "Your brother?" she croaked out in a husky whisper.

McClane sat on the bed. "Yes, Donavan was my brother. He was not my cousin as most people think. Wait, I should qualify the statement. He was my cousin *and* my brother. I shall tell you an obscure fact, a personal family secret. My Uncle Terrell was unable to produce issue. When Aunt Breanna discovered this, she knew she could not stay with him. She had desired to have a large family. Seven children were her goal - alternating boys and girls. She and Mother would become pregnant together, have children together and raise them together. The problem, though, was my mother was already pregnant with me. For Breanna to divorce Terrell and discover another man with a seven letter name, it would take too much precious time. So the four of them made a decision. It was brilliant, a truly masterful idea. My father impregnated Breanna. Unlike Terrell, his seed was potent. Unfortunately, Donavan and I were the only children as neither were able to conceive again. However, since my father's seed produced both children, my cousin is also my brother." His face clouded. "And he was taken from me." He picked up one of her shoes he had forced her to remove earlier and slammed it into the wall with enough force to leave a hole. He took a deep breath as if to calm himself and continued. "Donavan knew of my obsession with my garden, of course, he would. He knew everything about me just as I did about him. 'It's too dangerous to place your gift. Let me do it.'" McClane shook his head sadly. "When I heard the message on his answering machine telling him I had died and he would need to come identify the body, I knew such pain. Pain the likes of which I had never encountered before. Not even the agony of losing our parents so many years ago could come close to the emptiness of losing my brother. I managed to push the hollowness aside and realized this for the kismet it was. If I dared, I could use this horrible circumstance to complete my garden. Strange how fate works. I dressed in his clothes, marched right into the cold, sterile room and agreed they had destroyed Douglas McClane. We looked so much alike. His face was ruined. It was easy to fool them." He chortled at the duplicity of the officials. "But enough with the history lessons." He stood again and took her hand, pulling Joselyn until she stood. Running his hands over her form, he schooled himself in patience and ignored the raging desire to rush and consume her. Instead, he turned her and focused on the zipper running the length of her back. A groan erupted at the sight of her creamy skin. She was so ripe and ready. He had promised himself to go slow and enjoy this offering for his garden, but it had taken too long to obtain her. His soul couldn't wait. His body couldn't wait. His blade resting on the bed couldn't wait. It was time to make her his. He moaned as he reached for the zipper. "So lovely," he whispered reverently.

Chapter 25

Hold it together. Don't upset him. Wait for the police. Stay alive. Help is coming.

The words circled around and around in Joselyn's rattled mind. If she was honest with herself, she was not nearly as calm as the voice pretended. McClane activated the silent alarm when he came in so Detective Jameson and the New Orleans Police should be arriving at any moment. That is if he didn't know the new code. She mentally slammed the door on the thought. There was no way he would know it; she had to believe it. The monitoring company would wait one minute for the code to be turned off in case it was an accident. When the minute passed, they would notify the police. Given the traffic this time of day, it would take between twelve and eighteen minutes for them to arrive, another minute to get through the gate and then on to her house. Twenty minutes; she had to stall him for twenty minutes. Glancing at the clock again, she bit her lip. Eleven minutes had already passed. She hoped she could last another nine, but she wasn't sure she could. Already he was undressing her, touching her, licking her skin as it became visible to him. She thought of Betty downstairs in her little box and silently cursed one of Maddox's favorites. Cleaned or not, she should have kept the weapon with her, loaded and ready to go as he had taught her.

Maddox.

Crippling agony slammed into her at the memory of seeing his still body dangling from her wall. At first, she hadn't been able to understand what McClane was showing her. Then realization dawned on her, and she shattered. Maddox was dead? No! He couldn't be! He was too strong, right?

Her attention snapped back to the present moment as cool air caressed the bare skin of her back. Crossing her arms over her chest, she drew a ragged breath. "Please... please don't do this."

The chuckle sounding in her ear sent ice-cold daggers of terror straight to her heart. "You beg so prettily. I can't wait to hear your cries of terror. I'll drink each one from your lips like the finest of wine. There will be seven in total, one for each letter of our perfect names." He tugged her arms free, releasing the dress to fall at her feet in a puddle of deep amethyst. Grasping her chin, he held her face as he pulled her lips to his. Smashing them together, he forced her lips apart, thrusting his tongue deep inside. Her whimper of repulsion turned to a scream of pain. White-hot agony slammed into her as she felt something warm gush over her belly. Ripping herself away from him, she gasped to see a long ragged cut mar her left breast. Crimson welled up between her fingers as she tried to staunch the flow splattering on the carpet.

"Exquisite," he moaned, reaching down and starting to unzip his pants.

One moment she was staring in horror as his hand on his zipper, and in the next, she saw a blur as she was flung onto the bed. Bouncing once, she scrambled over the soft surface leaving red handprints behind until she slid off the other side. Curling against the wall, she fought off a wave of dizziness and nausea which threatened to swamp her. She gritted her teeth, grabbed a handful of tissues from the box on her nightstand and shoved them to her wound. Holding her palm against the deep cut pouring blood, she looked for McClane to see why he had not pounced on her.

She blinked. Surely the blood loss she was suffering was playing tricks on her eyes. On the other side of the bed, two men fought and grappled. The larger one, the one on top was as familiar to her as her name.

Maddox, oh dear God, her Maddox was alive, and he was currently beating the living crap out of Douglas McClane.

River hurt. His head ached, his throat burned and his fingers were almost broken, but he was alive. Thank God and Uncle Sam for his training. Throwing his hand up to grab the cord and keep it from crushing his windpipe had saved his life. Waking several minutes later with a horrible headache and blood dripping along his jaw from McClane's kick was better than the alternative. The same wouldn't be true for Joselyn's assailant when he got his hands on him. Movement caught his eye and he stiffened as Joselyn's terrified face appeared in the window of her bedroom. Behind her, he could make out another shape.

McClane.

Feigning death, River remained perfectly still and focused on breathing shallowly. Regretting the pain he knew this was causing her, he forced himself to stay motionless. McClane needed to think he was no longer a threat. Catching the murdering rapist off guard was his only hope.

When the two disappeared from the window, River pulled his leg up, dug under the cuff of his jeans and removed his Ka-bar. From there it was only a couple of swipes against the cord, and he was on the ground, tugging the rope from his throat and gasping breaths. Not taking the time to find his sidearm, he curled the Ka-bar in his fist and sprinted for the front door. His bruised fingers didn't want to hold his keys, and he almost dropped them twice before he could get the door open. Glancing at the panel, he saw the amber light indicating the silent alarm had been tripped. Good. The police would be here soon. If McClane was lucky, they might even get here fast enough to save his life. For everything he had put Joselyn through, Douglas McClane was going to die tonight if River got his way.

Leaving the door open, he crossed the entry, hurried past her office and took the stairs two at a time. Moving silently, he slowed as he reached the landing and listened. Inside, McClane was explaining how he was still alive, and Donovan was not. Brothers? Huh, he sure hadn't thought of that little twist. Pressing himself against the wall beside the door, River reached over and slowly turned the knob. It wasn't locked. Too damned easy.

He listened to the conversation a few more minutes and fury colored his vision a deep red. Taking several breaths to clear his head, he forced himself to remain calm. *Don't go in there half-cocked, Benson. Hold it together. You lose your shit and Joselyn will pay the price. Keep it together.*

All the wonderful advice he gave himself vanished the moment he heard her beg the bastard to stop. The callous reply from McClane had him shaking. *Calm. Stay in control. Wait. Wait.*

Every little pain racking his body disappeared when he heard Joselyn's muffled scream. In an instant, he was through the door. Taking in the scene for a split second, River registered the shocked look of disbelief on McClane's face and Joselyn's pale face as she slapped her hand over her bare chest. His body tensed like a coil when he realized she was completely naked and bleeding. Streams of blood welled between her fingers and splashed to the carpet beneath. His vision turned as scarlet as her blood. With a roar of rage, River slammed his shoulder into McClane, knocking him to the floor. In one smooth motion, he picked up Joselyn and tossed her on the bed out of harm's way. Maddox knelt over the man who dared to touch his woman and commenced to, as Uncle Aaron would say, 'Stomp a mudhole in his ass and walk it dry.'

Fists rained upon the body caught under him. Ignoring the flairs of pain from each slam of his injured hand, he reveled in the blood flying from McClane's nose and lip. He knew he should stop as his opponent lay unconscious but all he could see were the looks of terror on Joselyn's face, the words written on the side of the barn, her creamy skin as blood welled fort and her naked body being touched by this madman. His fists flew faster and harder as the thick stench of blood filled the air.

"Maddox?"

He ignored the sound of her voice. As long as McClane drew a breath, she was in danger. His knife -- he needed the Ka-bar. Stopping a moment, he looked around the floor for his blade. Movement caught his attention, and he zeroed in on Joselyn huddling in the corner.

"Please? Maddox," she whispered as her eyes rolled back and she slumped over. With the loss of pressure on her breast, the soaked paper she had used fell away, and warm blood ran sluggishly to land on the floor in fat red drops.

"Joselyn!" He bolted to his feet and flew to her. Gently he laid her prone on the floor. Grabbing the blanket off the end of her bed, he draped it over her bare body. He gathered a handful of the fabric and pressed it to her wound. "Joselyn? Honey, wake up. Please, I can't lose you, not now, not when I finally know what I want with the rest of my life. It's you, sweetheart. Everything else doesn't matter. I need you because you're the best part of me. I love you, honey." He pushed his head against her chest, holding his breath to listen for her heartbeat. Relief slid through him as he detected the faint, slow *whom-whom* signaling she was still alive; still here with him.

There was a sound behind him. River threw himself over Joselyn to partially cover her body and protect her from whatever was coming their way.

Looking behind him, he saw a monster stalking them. Fury etched on Douglas McClane's battered face as he lurched forward with River's Ka-bar clenched in his fist. Crimson spittle flew from his lip as he snarled.

Beautiful dreams in restful sleep,
but never to wake or repose in peace.
My beautiful rose, the day has come,
for you and your soldier's lives are done.

He lurched forward, and River threw up an arm to deflect the blade. Ignoring the searing bite of pain, he jerked when the loud report of gunfire echoed in the room. Douglas McClane's one unswollen eye widened in shock as he fell forward to land on his knees before toppling forward onto River.

"Violets are blue; roses are red, guess what asshole, now you're dead. And, by the way, he's a SEAL, not a damned Army grunt."

River would have laughed at Bull's impromptu poetry, but he didn't have the strength. "Bull, she's hurt," he croaked.

Bull pulled Douglas McClane's body off his friend and kicked a long black blade away. "So are you," he hissed and yelled over his shoulder to get the paramedics in here immediately. "Don't move. Stay still."

Looking down in confusion, River saw more blood pooling under his hip. Shock registered when he realized from where it originated. The hilt of his Ka-bar was sticking out of his side. McClane must have fallen on it as he died, pushing it into River's body. Funny, River didn't even feel it.

Until now.

Chapter 26

The irritating sounds of a television program dragged Joselyn from the dark arms of unconsciousness. Opening her eyes, she quickly shut them again. "Too bright," she whispered.

There was a click, and a hand took hers. "Joselyn?"

Cracking her eyelids again, she winced to see her mother's face, worry etched deeply into the lines around her eyes. Smacking her lips together, she tried to smile. "Hey, Mom."

"Oh thank God, baby." Mom lifted Joselyn's hand to her lips and kissed it. "We were so worried. Thirsty?"

Joselyn nodded, so Mom picked up a cup and placed the straw between her parched lips. "Sip a little bit. You've been out a while."

Taking a few sips, Joselyn laid back on the incredibly thin hospital pillow. Looking around, she frowned. Someone had placed a crystal vase full of roses on a small shelf on the wall. After everything she had been through, Joselyn was sure she would never be able to stand the sight or smell of the once favored flower again.

Catching her gaze, her mother smiled. "Aren't they beautiful? They are from your publisher."

"Please, can you get rid of them? Give them to the

nurse's station or throw them away. I don't want ever to see another rose as long as I live."

Understanding dawned on her mother. "Oh, of course, baby. I didn't think about it." She snatched the vase and walked out of the room. In a few moments, she was back. "There. Better?"

Joselyn nodded. "Have you met Maddox yet? Where is he? Probably getting coffee in the cafeteria, I suppose." The look on Mom's face made her stomach drop. "What's wrong? Where is he?"

Mom pulled a chair beside the bed and sat. "Honey, he was hurt, pretty badly. When they brought you both in last night, they couldn't get the bleeding to stop. I talked to his mother, Sarah. She dropped by to check on you a bit ago. She said he has two dislocated fingers, lots of bruises, a deep cut on one arm and a pretty bad stab wound. The knife punctured a kidney and severed the vessels. They tried to repair it, but it was too far gone, so they removed it."

Joselyn pulled the blanket off herself and threw her legs over the side.

"Wait, where do you think you're going?"

"I have to see him."

Mom shook her head. "You can't, baby. He's in ICU. Nobody can see him until at least ten a.m. this morning."

"Then I'll go wait until visiting hours. Mom, I have to go, please. I can't lay here waiting to hear how he is from someone else. Maddox is my life. He is everything to me. He came for me when I needed him most. If..." She swallowed and forced the words out. "If something happens, I have to be there. Please, Mom."

Mom studied her a moment and gave in. "Alright but I'm getting a wheelchair. You're still weak, and you don't need to pull your stitches open." She pulled a robe from the back of the door and grabbed Joselyn's slippers. Helping her daughter to thread her good arm through the robe, she draped it over her shoulder and tied the waist. Sliding Joselyn's feet into the slippers, Mom stood. "I can't believe you talked me into this," she mumbled and left the room in search of the required transportation.

Against her mother's better judgment, a chair was located, and she was carefully loaded into it, being mindful of her one arm still resting in a sling. One of her nurses, a romantic young woman who also happened to be a big fan of Joselyn's, helped her get settled and spread a light blanket over her lap. "Good luck," she said and opened the door.

The ICU waiting room was full. Aaron, Shaun, and Mr. Benson were standing in a corner talking quietly with Hannah leaning against Shaun's hip. Shaun had his hand buried in Hannah's auburn tresses, stroking her gently. Celia, Sarah and all four of Maddox's sisters were sitting in a group. When Joselyn was pushed into the room, Sarah jumped up and flew to Joselyn's side. "Are you alright, sweetie?"

"I'm fine, Sarah," she said and bit her lip when the woman's hug caused a slight tug on her wound. "How is he?"

"He hasn't come to yet. He lost a lot of blood, but

the doctor said he should be fine." She drew her arms around herself. "He looks so pale."

Bull crouched down beside her. "How are you doing, Joselyn?'

She gave him a tight smile. "I've been better. McClane?"

"Gone. He'll never bother you again."

The relief was profound; she felt the weight lift from her shoulders. "Really?"

He placed his hand on hers and gave it a slight squeeze. "Really. No trials, no more hiding, no more fear. It's all over."

"Thank God," she whispered and closed her eyes.

At 10:00, a chime sounded through the room. "Visitors are now allowed," a dulcet voice announced from a hidden speaker.

Everyone looked at her. Sarah stood and grabbed the handles of the chair. "Ready to see your man?" she asked and started to push her toward the door leading back to the unit.

Joselyn nodded. "More than anything on this Earth."

She gasped as they entered his room. Tubes and wires connected him to monitors and machines recording every minute detail of his body's functions. Sarah held Joselyn's hand as they talked quietly to him, asking him to open his eyes and talk to them. The allotted ten minutes passed quickly. With a heavy heart, Joselyn raised his hand and kissed his palm, promising to come back soon. She had tears in her eyes as Sarah returned her to the waiting room.

"Come on; you need a rest. You've lost a lot of blood. Let the others go see him, and you take a nap," Mom had insisted.

Joselyn didn't want to leave, but her body was so exhausted, her hands trembled. "Just a nap but I'll be back." She looked at Sarah. "You'll let me know if he wakes up?"

Sarah pressed a kiss to Joselyn's cheek. "Of course, honey. You go ahead and rest now."

Later that night, she was once again in the waiting room, watching the clock until time for the final visit for the evening at seven. The nap had done her good, as did a shower and clean clothes. Her doctor released her by three, but she returned to ICU. She wouldn't leave him. When visiting time was announced, she dutifully walked through the door again.

Returning from his side ten minutes later, she saw Detective Jameson talking with Aaron. Next to him stood three large men she had not seen before. Wrinkling her brow, she approached him.

"Hello, Detective Jameson."

"Joselyn, after all we have been through, you have the right to use my given name. Please call me Henry or even Bull." He glanced at the door behind her. "How is he?"

She shrugged. "The doctors say he's stable and improving, but he hasn't awakened yet. They say his body needs to heal and he'll wake up when he's ready. I wish he'd open his eyes if only for a minute so I can see for myself."

"River is strong, he'll be fine, you'll see. He'll be aggravating your socks off in no time."

She chuckled and glanced at the strangers behind him.

Catching her glance, he motioned for them to come forward. "Joselyn, I'd like you to meet Bruiser, Toad, and Cowboy, also known as Grayson Titus, Reese Harkins, and Alcide Montgomery. They're all members of River's team.

She stared at them. Obviously, the medications she was on loosened her tongue because she just came right out and said what went through her mind. "There's no such thing as an ugly SEAL is there? You're all big and sexy."

The room burst into laughter, and she blushed. "Oh crapadoo, I'm sorry," she apologized, chagrin making her face turn a bright red. "Medications," she admitted sheepishly.

"It's alright, Ma'am," Bruiser said and gave her a wink. "Bull called and told us about River. We got a few days leave so flew down to check on him. Unfortunately, Finch, Hick, and Railroad couldn't leave, but they are with him in thoughts."

She looked at the men who had been closer than anyone besides Shaun to Maddox and said with a watery smile. "Thank you for your service."

"Thank you for not giving up on him," Bruiser said gently.

"Never," she stated with resolve.

Something warm clutched at River's hand as he fought his way through the swampy darkness trying to claim him. He could hear someone speaking but couldn't untangle it from the background noise of electronic equipment and the *hiss* of air being fed into his lungs. Finally, he was able to pry one eye partially open and realized he was in a hospital room. Well, that made sense since everything in his body hurt.

He tried to lift a hand to push the oxygen tube from his nose, but a hand stopped him. "No, leave it alone," the soft voice admonished.

A buzz sounded too loud, and he winced. Another voice, asked, "May I help you?"

"He's awake," said the angelic tone.

That voice. He knew her voice.

Forcing both eyes open he looked around and spotted her. Sitting in a chair next to his bed was Joselyn. She wore a loose workout shirt and black yoga pants. One arm was resting in a sling. Her long blonde hair was up in a messy bun at the top of her head, and there was a strain around her eyes. The beautiful smile she gave he made his heart lurch.

"You're okay," he croaked.

"Yeah. I'm okay," she agreed, "and so will you be."

A nurse burst into his room, and Joselyn reluctantly let his hand go. After several moments of being poked, prodded and questioned, he was allowed some water. Yanking the cannula from his face, he rubbed his nose. Much better. That tube was irritating.

The nurse shook her head with a small laugh. "If you get light-headed, put it back on," she admonished. He promised he would although he had no intention of following through.

After the nurse disappeared, Joselyn returned to her seat.

"Your parents, Shaun, Hannah, and Marla are at my house. Aaron and Celia needed to get back to the farm, but I'll call them when you're ready. I'm glad you're finally awake. Bruiser, Toad, and Cowboy are hoping to see you before they leave to go back to California in the morning. They went to get some coffee."

"My team is here?"

"Of course they are. SEALs never leave SEALs behind. Not even after retirement."

He grinned. "How long was I out?"

"Couple of days, but you would come to for a few minutes then drift back to sleep. I'm guessing you don't remember any of it. They moved you out of ICU into this room yesterday. I was worried, but they said you would wake completely when you were ready. Typical of you. Doing everything on your own time."

"You know it."

He reached out and touched her face and groaned, letting his hand fall to the bed. "Jesus, what did they do to me?"

"I don't know if I'm the one to tell you."

He narrowed his eyes at her. "You're the perfect

one to tell me. What happened?"

Relenting, Joselyn told River everything she knew about the fight and the aftermath. He remembered most of it but some, thankfully, he didn't. When she finished, he nodded. "Down a kidney, eh? Think you can love a man with parts missing?" His tone was light, but there was a bit of apprehension in his question.

She stood, let the side rail fall and sat on the edge. Carefully as not to jostle him, she laid beside him and placed her head on his shoulder. "I love you exactly how you are. Doesn't matter to me if you're missing a kidney, a lung, a leg or whatever." She pressed a kiss to his chest. "Get some rest. There will be plenty of time to talk about all this later."

Wrapping his arm around her waist, he closed his eyes with a smile. Joselyn was in his arms, safe and sound.

Epilogue

Four months later

Joselyn's face felt like it was going to break from smiling so much. She watched Maddox as he stood on the stage, microphone in hand, belting out the lyrics of "My Girl" while his SEAL brothers executed perfect moves as his backup singers. Looking dashing in their dress whites, the six men had every eligible woman in the room panting. Truth be known, there were probably a couple of married ladies who were enjoying the show as well.

Married ladies. She sighed happily as she realized today she had joined their ranks. Glancing at the beautiful but simple platinum and diamond ring Maddox had placed on her hand a few hours ago, she felt her heart swell with love for this incredible man. Mrs. Maddox Benson. It had a nice ring to it.

Entering into the final chorus, her new husband dropped from the stage, advanced over to her and tugged her to her feet. With a swirl, he danced with her a moment before finishing the song, dipping her until her head almost touched the floor and kissing her soundly. Hoots and catcalls filled the air as she blushed.

Tossing the microphone toward the stage, Bruiser caught it in one hand and placed it with the others. Acting as emcee, he announced the next dance as a special dedication to Joselyn from Maddox and cued the DJ in the corner. The first few strains of Blake Shelton's "God Gave Me You" lifted into the air, and her breath hitched. Maddox swayed with her, whispering the words into her ear in his rich baritone. Lowering his head, he placed a kiss on her where a silvery scar showed above the décolletage of her grandmother's white silk wedding dress. She stilled in his arms. How lucky could one woman be? She was loved by this amazing man, and she returned that love with wholehearted abandon. She thought of the day her father placed his ring on her hand and her eyes misted. "Daddy would have loved you."

He hugged her close. "I'm sorry he couldn't be here today. I would do anything to take that hurt from you. I believe he's watching over you."

She sniffed quietly. "I know he is."

He gently wiped away the tears pooling in her eyes with one thumb. "Hey, this should be a happy day. "

She gazed up at him with every ounce of the love she felt in her heart. "It is the happiest day of my life."

When the song was done, he led her back to the head table and pulled the chair out for her before sitting beside. Lifting her hand to his lips, he pressed his lips to her knuckles before brushing them across his cheek.

Bunches of flowers filled the air with their fragrance with not a single rose in sight, much to her florist's chagrin. Her aversion to the once beloved flower had even affected Mom's rose bushes in her corner garden. Every time she saw the delicate pink petals, she shuddered with revulsion as visions of her destroyed bed assaulted her mind. Once Maddox was well enough, he quietly replaced both bushes with hydrangeas. The roses were taken to Mississippi where they now lived in a place of honor on the farm near the pond where Celia and Aaron were building a retirement cabin.

Following the simple but elegant ceremony with just family and a few close friends, Joselyn and Maddox celebrated their nuptials by throwing a huge lavish party. Yards of white bunting and twinkling miniature lights draped the ceiling and walls creating a magical setting. Dozens of tables crowned with elegant bunches of white magnolias, snowy gardenias, and baby's breath were scattered about the huge space. The dinner catered by Giovanni had been cleared away, leaving plenty of room for guests to mingle. In the back of the room, there was a white chocolate fountain surrounded by platters of fruit and cake for dipping. On the other side of the table was a cascade of another sort. Maddox had made a secret request to Giovanni, and the culinary artesian had come through. When Joselyn spotted the beautiful arrangement of crystal bowls simulating a waterfall containing green apple Happy Orchards candies she burst into laughter and hugged him tightly. It was perfect.

At the front of the room, directly behind the bride's table sat a huge wedding cake of smooth white fondant covered with hundreds of tiny edible pearls on a silver pedestal. The table next to it held a groom's cake shaped like a large SEALs trident pin being cut by Annabeth. Her riotous laughter filled the room as she took time between slices to flirt with Hick. Joselyn chuckled to herself. Annabeth had finally given up on trying to coerce Maddox into becoming a model. It looked like she now had her sights on another SEAL. Joselyn watched as Hick whispered something into Annabeth's ear, causing her face to flush as red as her hair. She pushed on his arm in mock horror, but her eyes were shining brightly. Grabbing a flute of champagne, she gulped it down. Picking up several napkins, she used them to fan herself. Interesting. Perhaps there was more than cake being discussed between those two.

Her musing was interrupted as the room echoed with calls from a couple of hundred guests crowded into the lavishly decorated ballroom housing their reception. "Speech! Speech!"

Kissing her knuckles again, Maddox rose and faced the room. Tapping on his champagne glass, he waited until the noise died down. Clearing his throat, he spoke.

"I spent twenty years serving my country in the Navy. When the time came to leave, I didn't know what I was going to do with the rest of my life. I knew a lot of brothers who went on to work in the private security sector or even the police force." He raised his glass toward Bull sitting nearby. "The only thing I knew before enlisting was how to work a farm, but given all the years of excitement I had lived, I wasn't sure if I could settle down again." He turned to look at Joselyn with love so pure, her heart stuttered in her chest. "Then I found my reason for living." Reverent *awws* filled the room as he continued. "I had no idea when I came to help a friend, I was walking into destiny. I had no clue sitting in the back booth of a coffee shop in downtown New Orleans was everything I could ever hope or dream of. Looking back, I wonder how you put up with me. Grouchy, cold - you even nicknamed me Frost Giant. I was so determined not to get involved. I would be frosty, clinical, reserved and get the job done." He chuckled. "It was a lost cause. With the first glimpse, I was hooked. Every time you stood up to me, that fire showed in every word you spoke. I felt a little more of the frost melt. When you showed confidence in me, I found I can do anything. Well, anything except deny you whatever you wanted. Joselyn, you did the impossible. You stole my heart and tucked it away deep inside of you. It's yours. It has always been yours, and I never want it back again. Everything I ever can be is found in your eyes." He knelt beside her and placed her hand on his chest. "This is all yours, forever. I love you, Joselyn Benson."

Applause erupted from the gathered throng as he touched his lips to hers. Just like always, flames of heat licked her body, and she trembled. He growled softly. "Later, love. Just a couple more hours and we can leave this shindig." He gave her a saucy wink and stood with a fiery passion burning in his eyes. She was happy she wasn't the only one affected by the smoking hot chemistry between them.

The DJ started another song, and soon the dance floor was filled with laughing people moving to the beat of a pop tune. A throat cleared, catching her attention and she smiled at Aaron standing behind them. Pulling a chair out, Maddox motioned to it. "Hey, Uncle Aaron. Have a seat." Picking his bride up, he sat in her chair and settled her into his lap. Kissing the nape of her neck, he rested his chin on her shoulder.

The older man hesitated and dropped into the chair. Pulling out an envelope, he pushed it into Maddox's hands. "I wanted to give you two our gift."

Opening the envelope, Maddox pulled out a stack of papers. His brow wrinkled as he looked them over and shock registered. "We can't take this."

"You can and you will. The cabin on the lake is almost finished. We'll be moving out there and retiring on ten or so acres. Shaun and Hannah will stay in the big house." He jabbed a finger at the paper. "This deed is for the old homestead and forty acres on the west side of the property. You always loved that piece of land, so it's only fitting you get it. You and Shaun have been taking about restarting the breeding program. I also know you're concerned about the distance between Meridian and New Orleans. Now, you don't have to worry about it. Joselyn has assured me she can work from anywhere in the world so there you go. I reckon you'll have to get a decent internet service out there, but I'll leave it to you."

Maddox swallowed. Gently nudging Joselyn from his lap, he stood as Aaron did and hugged the man tightly. "Thank you," he said simply.

"Family," he stated with a shrug as if that was the answer to any question. He kissed Joselyn's astonished face and rejoined his wife and sister at their table nearby.

Maddox stared at the deed in his hand and then at her. "I guess we need to talk about this. I mean, we have been spending a lot of time on the farm lately, but this is permanent."

She cut him off. "You and Shaun spend loads of time on Skype talking about the possibilities for a new breeding program. That tells me you're both wanting to get it started. Honey, I'm not blind. I see how happy it makes you there on the farm. It's where you need to be, and I want to be by your side. Aaron is right. I can write from anywhere. You need to be where your heart is."

He dropped the papers on the table, grabbed her by the waist and pulled her into his lap. "That's easy, then. My heart is where you are. You've given me a precious gift. Your love means more to me than anything on this Earth. I'll protect and cherish it every day for the rest of my life. I'll never let anything happen to it or you. I swear to protect you, Joselyn."

"Forever."

Thank you for taking the time to read *Protecting Joselyn*. This is the first book in my Team Cerberus SEALs series. Each book is a stand alone novel complete with lots of twists and turns but ending with a happily ever after. If you enjoyed the book, please take a moment to leave a review – even if it's just a line or two. It's much appreciated!

The next book in this series is **Saving Olivia**. It's the story of Grayson "Bruiser" Titus and his lady, Oliva Parker. He's the leader of the team who never knew a family until he joined the SEALs. She's the product of a broken home who just wants to do what's right for herself and her brother. Unfortunately, she catches the eye of a collector of women and is captured and sold. Now it's up to Bruiser and his team to find and save her.

Read what happens next in **Saving Olivia**, available at Amazon and in Kindle Unlimited.

Happy Reading!

About the Author

I was born in Tupelo, Mississippi and raised in Houlka, a small rural town forty-five minutes southwest down the famous Natchez Trace. Living in the country with no close neighbors guaranteed I would develop an over active imagination. I didn't have playmates so often made my own up including backstories and lives of their own. I spent hours daily playing games with them, building sand castles for them to live in, and taking them "swimming" in the mud holes of the soybean fields surrounding our home. That imagination would become a love for creating my own worlds.

It wasn't until college that I tried to write my first novel. Unfortunately, it was quite bad and became lost in the shuffle of transitioning between teenager to adult. This minor failure didn't deter my desire to write - it just cooled it for a while. That fire was rekindled in 2012 with the death of a close friend who also aspired to become an author. Robin's passing reminded me that life is too short to ignore your dreams. Because of her, I sat down, determined to finish one book and publish it. Less than a year later, I achieved that goal by publishing Shattered Dreams. My only regret is not being able to share this ride with her. I know if she was here, she would be in the mix of it with me.

Love you, Robin, Mean it!

Several years and many novels later, I continue to pen my stories covering several genres from paranormal to romantic suspense. I currently reside in Meridian, Mississippi with my very supportive family - husband Robert and daughter Rebecca. When I'm not sweating over a new story, I enjoy reading everything I can, talking to my friends all over the world, honing my skills as a YouTube connoisseur, and being bossed around by my pet conure, Poppy.

Website: https://www.mkclarke.com
Facebook: https://www.facebook.com/Melissakayclarke/
Twitter : https://twitter.com/MelissaKayClark
Blog: https://melissakayclarke.wordpress.com/
Instagram: @mkclarke
BookBub: https://www.bookbub.com/authors/melissa-kay-clarke

Other Works

Luna's Children
Shattered Dreams
Broken Melody
Lorestone: The Strength Within

The Legacy Reborn
Reclamation

Team Cerberus
Protecting Joselyn
Saving Olivia
Defending Demma *(paperback)*
Rescuing Annabeth
Safeguarding Miley
Justice for Breeze
Safeguarding Ara
Shielding Evanleigh

G.E.M.S.
Diamond *(Coming July 21, 2020)*
Emerald
Ruby
Sapphire
Topaz

Hometown Heroes
Harmony in the Key of Murder *(paperback)*
Deadly Impressions

Anthologies
Defending Demma
(a Team Cerberus novella available in Can't Buy Me Love)
Harmony in the Key of Murder
(a Hometown Heroes novella available in Once Upon a Summer)

Made in the USA
Monee, IL
14 June 2020